In Her Shoes

Modern-day Cinderellas get their grooms!

Now you can with this new miniseries
from Harlequin® Romance that's
brimming full of contemporary, feel-good stories.

Our modern-day Cinderellas
swap glass slippers for stylish stilettos!

So follow each footstep through makeover to marriage
and rags to riches, as these women
fulfill their hopes and dreams....

Look out for more In Her Shoes stories
coming soon!

JESSICA STEELE

The Girl from Honeysuckle Farm

In Her Shoes

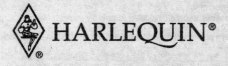

HARLEQUIN®

TORONTO • NEW YORK • LONDON
AMSTERDAM • PARIS • SYDNEY • HAMBURG
STOCKHOLM • ATHENS • TOKYO • MILAN • MADRID
PRAGUE • WARSAW • BUDAPEST • AUCKLAND

Recycling programs
for this product may
not exist in your area.

ISBN-13: 978-0-373-17634-2

THE GIRL FROM HONEYSUCKLE FARM

First North American Publication 2010.

Copyright © 2009 by Jessica Steele.

This edition published by arrangement with Harlequin Books S.A.

www.eHarlequin.com

Printed in U.S.A.

Jessica Steele lives in the county of Worcestershire, with her super husband, Peter, and their gorgeous Staffordshire bull terrier, Florence. Any spare time is spent enjoying her three main hobbies: reading espionage novels, gardening (she has a great love of flowers) and playing golf. Any time left over is celebrated with her fourth hobby: shopping. Jessica has a sister and two brothers, and they all, with their spouses, often go on golfing holidays together. Having traveled to various places around the globe to research backgrounds for her stories, there are many countries she would like to revisit. Her most recent trip abroad was to Portugal, where she stayed in a lovely hotel, close to her all-time favorite golf course. Jessica had no idea of being a writer until one day Peter suggested she write a book. So she did. She has now written more than eighty novels.

Happy New Year!

Welcome to 2010 and another year of fabulous, feel-good reads from Harlequin Romance.

This month, get swept up in *The Italian's Forgotten Baby* by **Raye Morgan.** An idyllic island and an irresistible Italian recapturing lost memories make for a real page-turner! Fasten your seat belt as your ESCAPE AROUND THE WORLD continues—on the arm of a gorgeous Mediterranean man in a hot-air balloon in sunny Spain! The warmth and emotion of **Barbara McMahon**'s *The Daredevil Tycoon* will leave your senses tingling!

If you'd rather keep your feet firmly on the ground perhaps you'll accept an invitation to the weddings of the year.... **Cara Colter** and **Shirley Jump** bring you *Just Married!*: two linked stories in one volume for double the chance to catch the bouquet!

After all that excitement, curl up and relax with a laid-back cowboy in **Donna Alward**'s heartwarming tale *One Dance with the Cowboy,* the first in her brand-new duet COWBOYS & CONFETTI. Then from the Rocky Mountains to the rolling hills of the English countryside, **Jessica Steele**'s perfect English gentleman will steal your heart in *The Girl from Honeysuckle Farm.*

If you love Jessica Steele, don't miss the warm, witty and wildly romantic *Hired: Sassy Assistant* by sparkling new talent **Nina Harrington.**

Which will you read first?

CHAPTER ONE

PHINN tried hard to look on the bright side—but could not find one. There was not so much as a glimmer of a hint of a silver lining to the dark cloud hanging over her.

She stared absently out of the window of her flat above the stables, barely noticing that Geraldine Walton, the new owner of the riding school, while somehow managing to look elegant even in jeans and a tee shirt, was already busy organising the day's activities.

Phinn had been up early herself, and had already been down to check on her elderly mare Ruby. Phinn swallowed down a hard lump in her throat and came away from the window, recalling the conversation she'd had with Kit Peverill yesterday. Kit was Ruby's vet, and he had been as kind as he could be. But, however kind he had been, he could not minimise the harshness that had to be faced when he told her that fragile Ruby would not see the year out.

Phinn was quite well aware that Ruby had quite a few health problems, but even so she had been very shaken. It was already the end of April. But, however shaken she had been, her response had been sharp when he had suggested that she might want to consider allowing him to put Ruby down.

'No!' she had said straight away, the idea not needing to be considered. Then, as she'd got herself more collected,

'She's not in great pain, is she? I mean, I know you give her a painkilling injection occasionally, but...'

'Her medication is keeping her relatively pain-free,' Kit had informed her. And Phinn had not needed to hear any more. She had thanked him for his visit and had stayed with Ruby for some while, reflecting how Ruby had been her best friend since her father had rescued the mare from being ill treated thirteen years ago, and had brought her home.

But, while they had plenty of space at Honeysuckle Farm in which to keep a horse, there had been no way they could afford to keep one as a pet.

Her mother, already the breadwinner in the family, had hit the roof. But equally there had been no way that Ewart Hawkins was going to let the emaciated mare go back to the people he had rescued her from. And since he had threatened—and had meant it—to have them prosecuted if they tried to get her back, her owners had moved on without her.

'Please, Mummy,' Phinn remembered pleading, and her mother had looked into her pleading blue eyes, so like her own, and had drawn a long sigh.

'You'll have to feed and water her, *and* clean up after her,' she had said severely. 'Daily!'

And Ewart, the battle over, had given his wife a delighted kiss, and Phinn had exchanged happy grins with her father.

She had been ten years old then, and life had been wonderful. She had been born on the farm to the best parents in the world. Her childhood, given the occasional volcanic explosions from her mother when Ewart had been particularly outrageous about something, had been little short of idyllic. Any major rows between her parents, she'd later realised had, in the main, been kept from her.

Her father had adored her from the word go. Because of some sort of complication at her birth, her mother had had to stay in bed, and it had been left to Ewart to look after the newborn. They had lived in one of the farm cottages then, only moving to the big farmhouse when Grandfather and then Grandmother Hawkins had died. Phinn's father had bonded with his baby daughter immediately, and, entirely uninterested in farming, he had spent hour after hour with his little girl. It had been he who, advised by his wife, Hester, that the child had to be registered with the authorities within forty-two days of her birth, had gone along to the register office with strict instructions to name her Elizabeth Maud—Maud after Hester's mother.

He had never liked his mother-in-law, and had returned home to have to explain himself to his wife.

'You've called her—*what*?' Hester had apparently hit a C above top C.

'Calm down, my love,' he had attempted to soothe, and had gone on to explain that with a plain name like Hawkins, he had thought the baby had better have a pretty name to go in front.

'Delphinium!'

'I'm not having my beautiful daughter called plain Lizzie Hawkins,' he'd answered, further explaining, 'To be a bit different I've named her Delphinnium, with an extra "n" in the middle.' And, to charm his still not mollified wife, 'I'm rather hoping little Phinn will have your gorgeous delphinium-blue eyes. Did you know,' he went on, 'that your beautiful eyes go all dark purple, like the Black Knight delphinium, when you're all emotional?'

'Ewart Hawkins,' she had threatened, refusing to be charmed.

'And I brought you a cabbage,' he'd said winningly.

The fact that he had brought it, not bought it, had told her that he had nipped over some farmer's hedge and helped himself.

'Ewart Hawkins!' she'd said again, but he had the smile he had wanted.

Hester Rainsworth, as she had been prior to her marriage,

had been brought up most conventionally in a workaholic family. Impractical dreamer, talented pianist, sometime poet and would-be mechanical engineer Ewart Hawkins could not have been more of an opposite. They had fallen in love—and for some years had been blissfully happy.

Given a few ups and downs, it had been happiness all round in Phinn's childhood. Grandfather Hawkins had been the tenant of the farm, and on his death the tenancy had passed to her father. The farm had then been her father's responsibility, but after one year of appalling freak weather, when they had spent more than they had earned, Hester had declared that, with money tight, Ewart could be farmer and house-husband too, while she went out and found a job and brought some money in.

Unlike his hard-working practical father, Ewart had had little interest in arable farming, and had seen absolutely no point in labouring night and day only to see his crops flattened by storms. Besides, there'd been other things he'd preferred to do. Teach his daughter to sketch, to fish, to play the piano and to swim just for starters. There was a pool down at Broadlands, the estate that owned both Honeysuckle Farm and the neighbouring Yew Tree Farm. They hadn't been supposed to swim in the pool, but in return for her father going up to the Hall occasionally, and playing the grand piano for music-lover Mr Caldicott, old Mr Caldicott had turned a blind eye.

So it was in the shallows there that her father had taught her to dive and to swim. If they hadn't taken swimwear it had been quite all right with him if she swam in her underwear—and should his wife be home when they returned, he'd borne her wrath with fortitude.

There was a trout stream too, belonging to the Broadlands estate, and they hadn't been supposed to fish there either. But her father had called that a load of nonsense, so fish they had. Though, for all Phinn had learned to cast a fine line, she could never kill a fish and her fish had always been put back. Afterwards they might stop at the Cat and Drum, where her father would sit her outside with a lemonade while he went inside to pass time with his friends. Sometimes he would bring his pint outside. He would let her have a sip of his beer and, although she thought it tasted horrible, she had pretended to like it.

Phinn gave a shaky sigh as she thought of her dreamer father. It had been he and not her mother who had decorated her Easter bonnet for the village parade. How proud she had been of that hat—complete with a robin that he had very artistically made.

'A robin!' her mother had exclaimed. 'You do *know* it's Easter?'

'There won't be another bonnet like it,' he had assured her.

'You can say that again!' Hester had retorted.

Phinn had not won the competition. She had not wanted to. Though she had drawn one or two stares, it had not mattered. Her father had decorated her hat, and that had been plenty good enough for her.

Phinn wondered, not for the first time, when it had all started to go so badly wrong. Had it been before old Mr Caldicott had decided to sell the estate? Before Ty Allardyce had come to Bishops Thornby, taken a look around and decided to buy the place—thereby making himself their landlord? Or…?

In all fairness, Phinn knew that it must have been long before then. Though he, more recently, had not helped. Her beautiful blue eyes darkened in sadness as she thought back to a time five, maybe six years ago. Had that been when things had started to go awry? She had come home after having been out for a ride with Ruby, and after attending to Ruby's needs she had gone into the big old farmhouse kitchen to find her parents in the middle of a blazing row.

Knowing that she could not take sides, she had been about to back out again when her mother had taken her eyes from the centre of her wrath—Ewart—to tell her, 'This concerns you too, Phinn.'

'Oh,' she had murmured non-committally.

'We're broke. I'm bringing in as much as I can.' Her mother worked in Gloucester as a legal assistant.

'I'll get a job,' Phinn had offered. 'I'll—'

'You will. But first you'll have some decent training. I've arranged for you to have an interview at secretarial college. You—'

'She won't like it!' Ewart had objected.

'We all of us—or most of us,' she'd inserted, with a sarcastic glance at him, 'have to do things we don't want to do or like to do!'

The argument, with Phinn playing very little part, had raged on until Hester Hawkins had brought out her trump card.

'Either Phinn goes to college or that horse goes to somebody who can afford her feed, her vet and her farrier!'

'I'll sell something,' Ewart had decided, already not liking that his daughter, his pal, would not be around so much. He had a good brain for anything mechanical, and the farmyard was littered with odds and ends that he would sometimes make good and sell on.

But Hester had grown weary of him. 'Grow up, Ewart,' she had snapped bluntly.

But that was the trouble. Her father had never grown up, and had seen no reason why he should attempt it. On thinking about it, Phinn could not see any particular reason why he should have either. Tears stung her eyes. Though it had been the essential Peter Pan in her fifty-four-year-old father that had ultimately been the cause of his death.

But she did not want to dwell on that happening seven months ago. She had shed enough tears since then.

Phinn made herself think back to happier times, though she had not been too happy to be away from the farm for such long hours while she did her training. For her mother's sake she had applied herself to that training, and afterwards, with her eye more on the salary she would earn than with any particular interest in making a career as a PA, she had got herself a job with an accountancy firm, with her mother driving her into Gloucester each day.

Each evening Phinn had got home as soon as she could to see Ruby and her father. Her father had taught her to drive, but when her mother had started working late, putting in extra hours at her office, it was he who had suggested that Phinn should have a car of her own.

Her mother had agreed, but had insisted *she* would look into it. She was not having her daughter driving around in any bone-rattling contraption he'd patched up.

Phinn had an idea that Grandmother Rainsworth had made a contribution to her vehicle, and guessed that her mother's parents might well have helped out financially in her growing years.

But all that had stopped a few months later when her mother, having sat her down and said that she wanted to talk to her, had announced to Phinn's utter amazement that she was moving out. Shocked, open-mouthed, Phinn had barely taken in that her mother intended leaving them when she'd further revealed that she had met someone else.

'You mean—some—other man?' Phinn had gasped, it still not fully sinking in.

'Clive. His name's Clive.'

'But—but what about Dad?'

'I've discussed this fully with your father. Things—er—haven't been right between us for some while. I'll start divorce proceedings as soon as everything settles…'

Divorce! Phinn had been aware that her mother had grown

more impatient and short-tempered with her father just lately. But—*divorce*!

'But what—'

'I'm not going to change my mind, Phinn. I've tried. Lord knows I've tried! But I'm tired of the constant struggle. Your father lives in his own little dream world and…' She halted at the look of protest on her daughter's face. 'No, I'm not going to run him down. I know how devoted you are to him. But just try to understand, Phinn. I'm tired of the struggle. And I've decided I'm not too old to make a fresh start. To make a new life for myself. A better life.'

'Th-this Clive. He's part of your fresh start—this better life?'

'Yes, he is. In due time I'll marry him—though I'm not in any great hurry about that.'

'You—just want your—freedom?'

'Yes, I do. You're working now, Phinn. You have your own money—though no doubt your father will want some of it. But…' Hester looked at her daughter, wanting understanding. 'I've found myself a small flat in Gloucester. I'll write down the address. I'm leaving your father, darling, not you. You're welcome to come and live with me whenever you want.'

To leave her father had been something Phinn had not even thought about. Her home had been there, with him and Ruby.

It was around then, Phinn suddenly saw, that everything had started to go wrong.

First Ruby had had a cough, and when that cleared she'd picked up a viral infection. Her father had been marvelous, in that he'd spent all of his days looking after Ruby for her until Phinn was able to speed home from the office to take over.

The vet's bill had started to mount, but old Mr Duke had obligingly told them to pay what they could when they could.

Phinn's days had become full. She'd had no idea of the amount of work her mother had done when she was home. Phinn had always helped out when requested, but once she was sole carer she'd seemed to spend a lot of her time picking up and clearing up after her father.

And time had gone by. Phinn had met Clive Gillam and, contrary to her belief, had liked him. And a couple of years later, with her father's approval, she had attended their wedding.

'You want to go and live with them?' her father had asked somewhat tentatively when she had returned.

'No way,' she'd answered.

And he had grinned. 'Fancy a pint?'

'You go. I want to check on Rubes.'

It seemed as though her mother's new marriage had been a signal for everything to change. Mr Caldicott, the owner of the Broadlands estate, had decided to sell up and to take himself and his money off to sunnier climes.

And, all before they knew it, the bachelor Allardyce brothers had been in the village, taking a look around. And, all before they could blink, Honeysuckle Farm and neighbouring Yew Tree Farm, plus a scattering of other properties, had all had a new landlord—and an army of architects and builders had started at work on Broadlands Hall, bringing its antiquated plumbing and heating up to date and generally modernising the interior.

She had spotted the brothers one day when she was resting Ruby, hidden in the spinney—property of Broadlands. Two men deep in conversation had walked by. The slightly taller of the two, a dark-haired man, just had to be the Tyrell Allardyce she had heard about. There was such a self-confident air about the man that he could have been none other than the new owner.

Phinn had seemed to know that before she'd overheard his deep, cultured tones saying, 'Don't you see, Ash...?' as they had passed within yards of her.

Ash was tall too, but without that positive, self-assured air that simply exuded from the other man. Listening intently, he must have been the younger brother.

Tyrell Allardyce, with his brother Ashley, had called at Honeysuckle Farm one day while she was out at work. But from what her father had told her, and from what she had gleaned from the hotbed of local gossip, Ty Allardyce was some big-shot financier who worked and spent most of his time either in London or overseas. He, so gossip had said, would live at Broadlands Hall when his London commitments allowed, while Ashley would stay at the Hall to supervise the alterations and generally manage the estate.

'Looks like we're going to be managed, kiddo,' her father had commented jocularly.

Highly unlikely!

Further village gossip some while later had suggested that Mrs Starkey, housekeeper to the previous owner of Broadlands, was staying on to look after Ashley Allardyce. It seemed—though Phinn knew that, village gossip being what it was, a lot of it could be discounted—that Ashley had endured some sort of a breakdown, and that Ty had bought Broadlands mainly for his brother's benefit.

Phinn thought she could safely rule that out—the cost of Broadlands, with all its other properties, must go into millions. Surely, if it were true that Ashley had been ill, there were cheaper ways of finding somewhere less fraught than London to live? Though it did appear that the younger Allardyce brother *was* living at the Hall. So perhaps Mrs Starkey, whom Phinn had known all her life, was looking after him after all.

Everything within this last year seemed to be changing. To start with, old Mr Duke had decided to give up his veterinary practice. It was a relief that she had just about settled with him the money she'd owed for Ruby's last course of treatment. Though it had worried Phinn how she would fare with the new man who had taken over. Mr Duke had never been in any hurry for his money, and Ruby, who they calculated had been about ten years old when they had claimed her, was now geriatric in the horse world, and rarely went six weeks without requiring some treatment or other.

Kit Peverill, however, a tall mousy-haired man in his early thirties, had turned out to be every bit as kind and caring as his predecessor. Thankfully, she had only had to call him out twice.

But more trouble had seemed to be heading their way when, again clearing up after her father, she'd found a letter he had left lying around. It had come from the Broadlands estate, and was less of a letter but more of a formal notice that some effort must be made to pay the rent arrears and that the farm must be 'tidied up'—otherwise legal proceedings would have to be initiated.

Feeling staggered—she'd had no idea that her father had not been paying the rent—Phinn had gone in search of him.

'Ignore it,' he had advised.

'Ignore it?' she'd gasped.

'Not worth the paper it's written on,' he had assured her, and had gone back to tinkering with an old, un-roadworthy, un-fieldworthy quad bike he had found somewhere.

Knowing that she would get no sense out of him until his mind-set was ready to think of other things, Phinn had waited until he came into supper that night.

'I was thinking of going down to the Cat for a pint—' he began.

'I was thinking we might discuss that letter,' Phinn interrupted.

He looked at her, smiled because he adored her, and said, 'You know, little flower, you've more than a touch of your mother about you.'

She couldn't ignore it. One of them had to be practical. 'What will we do if—er—things get nasty—if we have to leave here? Ruby...'

'It won't come to that,' he'd assured her, undaunted. 'It's just the new owner flexing a bit of muscle, that's all.'

'The letter's from Ashley Allardyce...'

'He may have written it, but he will have been instructed by his big brother.'

'Tyrell Allardyce.' She remembered him very clearly. Oddly, while Ashley Allardyce was only a vague figure in her mind, his elder brother Ty seemed to be etched in her head. She was starting to dislike the man.

'It's the way they do things in London,' Ewart had replied confidently. 'They just need all the paperwork neatly documented in case there's a court case. But—' as she went a shade pale '—it won't come to that,' he repeated. 'Honeysuckle Farm has been in Hawkins care for generations. Nobody's going to throw us off this land, I promise you.'

Sadly, it had not been the first letter of that sort. The next one she had seen had come from a London firm of lawyers, giving them formal notice to quit by September. And Phinn, who had already started to dislike Tyrell Allardyce, and although she had never hated anyone in her life, had known that she hated Ty that he could do this to them. Old Mr Caldicott would never, ever have instructed such a letter.

But again her father had been unconcerned, and told her to ignore the notice to quit. And while Phinn had spent a worrying time—expecting the bailiffs to turn up at any moment to turf then out—her father had appeared to not have a care in the world.

And then it had been September, and Phinn had had something else to worry about that had pushed her fear of the bailiffs into second place. Ruby had become quite ill.

Kit Peverill had come out to her in the middle of the night, and it had been touch and go if Ruby would make it. Phinn, forgetting she had a job to go to, had stayed with her and nursed her, watched her like a hawk—and the geriatric mare had pulled through.

When Phinn had gone back to work and, unable to lie, told

her boss that her mare had been ill, she had been told in return that they were experiencing a business downturn and were looking to make redundancies. Was it likely, should her horse again be ill, that she would again take time off?

Again she had not been able to lie. 'I'll go and clear my desk,' she'd offered.

'You don't have to go straight way,' her employer had told her kindly. 'Let's say in a month's time.'

Because she'd known she would need the money, Phinn had not argued. But she never did work that full month. Because a couple of weeks later her world had fallen apart when her father, haring around the fields, showing a couple of his pals what a reconstructed quad bike could do, had upended it, gone over and under it—and come off worst.

He had died before Phinn could get to the hospital. Her mother had come to her straight away, and it had been Hester who, practical to the last, had made all the arrangements.

Devastated, having to look after Ruby had been the only thing that kept Phinn on anything resembling an even keel. And Ruby, as if she understood, would gently nuzzle into her neck and cuddle up close.

Her father had been popular but, when the day of his funeral had arrived, Phinn had never known he had so many friends. Or relatives, either. Aunts and uncles she had heard of but had seen only on the rarest of occasions had come to pay their respects. Even her cousin Leanne, a Hawkins several times removed, had arrived with her parents.

Leanne was tall, dark, pretty—and with eyes that seemed to instantly put a price on everything. But since the family antiques had been sold one by one after Hester had left, there had been very little at Honeysuckle Farm that was worth the ink on a price ticket. Thereafter Leanne had behaved as decorously as her parents would wish.

That was she'd behaved very nicely until—to his credit—

Ashley Allardyce had come to the funeral to pay his respects too. Phinn had not been feeling too friendly to him, but because she did not wish to mar the solemnity of the occasion with any undignified outburst—and in any case it was not him but his elder brother Ty who was the villain who went around instigating notices to quit—she'd greeted Ashley calmly, and politely thanked him for coming.

Leanne, noticing the expensive cut of the clothes the tall, fair-haired man was wearing, had immediately been attracted.

'Who's he?' she'd asked, sidling up when Ashley Allardyce had gone over to have a word with Nesta and Noel Jarvis, the tenants of Yew Tree Farm.

'Ashley Allardyce,' Phinn had answered, and, as she'd suspected, it had not ended there.

'He lives around here?'

'At Broadlands Hall.'

'That massive house in acres of grounds we passed on the way here?'

The next thing Phinn knew was that Leanne, on her behalf, had invited Ash Allardyce back to the farmhouse for refreshments.

Any notion Phinn might have had that he would refuse the invitation had disappeared when she'd seen the look on his face. He was clearly captivated by her cousin!

The days that had followed had gone by in a numbed kind of shock for Phinn as she'd tried to come to terms with her father's death. Her mother had wanted her to go back to Gloucester and live with her and Clive. Phinn had found the idea unthinkable. Besides, there was Ruby.

Phinn had been glad to have Ruby to care for. Glad too that her cousin Leanne frequently drove the forty or so miles from her own home to see her.

In fact, by the time Christmas had come, Phinn had seen more of her cousin than she had during the whole of her life.

Leanne had come, she would say, to spend time with her, so she would not be too lonely. But most of Leanne's time, from what Phinn had seen, was being spent with Ash Allardyce.

He had driven Leanne back to the farmhouse several times, and it had been as clear as day to Phinn that he was totally besotted with her cousin. Phinn, aware, if village talk were true, of his recent recovery from a breakdown, had only hoped that, vulnerable as he might still be, he would not end up getting hurt.

Because of a prior arrangement Leanne had spent Christmas skiing in Switzerland. Ash had gone too. For all Phinn knew his notice-to-quit-ordering brother might have made one of his rare visits to Broadlands and spent his Christmas there, but she hadn't seen him, and she'd been glad about that. The notice to quit had never been executed. It had not needed to be.

Since Phinn had no longer had a job, she'd no longer needed a car. Pride as much as anything had said she had to clear the rent arrears. She had formed a good opinion of Ash Allardyce, and did not think he would discuss their business with Leanne, but with him becoming closer and closer to her cousin, she had not wanted to risk it. She did not want any one member of her family to know that her father had died owing money. She'd sold her car and sent a cheque off to the lawyers.

Though by the time all accounts had been settled—and that included the vet's last bill—there had been little money remaining, and Phinn had known that she needed to get a job. A job that paid well. Yet Ruby had not been well enough to be left alone all day while she went off to work.

Then Leanne, on another visit, having voiced her opinion that Ash was close to 'popping the question' marriage-wise, had telephoned from Broadlands Hall to tell her not to wait up for her, that she was spending the night there.

It had been the middle of the following morning when Leanne, driving fast and furiously, had screeched to a halt in the middle of the farmyard. Phinn, leaving Ruby to go and find out what the rush was about, had been confronted by a furious Leanne, who'd demanded to know why she had not told her that Broadlands Hall did *not* belong to Ash Allardyce.

'I—didn't think about it,' Phinn had answered defensively. Coming to terms with her beloved father's death and settling his affairs had taken precedence. Who owned Broadlands Hall had not figured very much, if at all, in her thinking at that particular time. 'I told you Ash had a brother. I'm sure I did.'

'Yes, you did!' Leanne snapped. 'And so did Ash. But neither of you told me that Ash was the *younger* brother—and that he doesn't own a *thing*!'

'Ah, you've met Ty Allardyce,' Phinn realised. And discovered she was in the wrong about that too.

'No—more's the pity! He's always away somewhere—away abroad somewhere, and likely to be away some time!' Leanne spat. 'It took that po-faced housekeeper to delight in telling me that Ash was merely the estate *manager*! Can you imagine it? There was I, happily believing that any time soon I was going to be mistress of Broadlands Hall, only to be informed by some jumped-up housekeeper that some poky farm cottage was more likely to be the place for me. I don't think so!'

Phinn doubted that Mrs Starkey would have said anything of the sort, but as Leanne raged on she knew that once her cousin had realised that Ash was not the owner of Broadlands, it wouldn't have taken her very long to realise the ins and outs of it all.

'Come in and I'll make some coffee,' Phinn offered, aware that her cousin had suffered something of a shock.

'I'll come in. But only to collect what belongings of mine I've left here.'

'You—er—that sounds a bit—final?' Phinn suggested at last.

'You bet it is. Ten minutes and the village of Bishop Thornby has seen the last of me.'

'What about Ash?'

'What about him?' Leanne was already on her way into the house. 'I've told him—nicely—that I'm not cut out for country life. But if that hasn't given him something of a clue—tell him I said goodbye.'

Ash did not come looking for her cousin, and Honeysuckle Farm had settled into an unwanted quietness. With the exception of her mother, who frequently rang to check that she was all right, Phinn spoke with no one other than Ruby. Gradually Phinn came to see that she could do nothing about Leanne having dropped Ash like a hot brick once she had known that he was not the one with the money. Phinn knew that she could not stay on at the farm for very much longer. She had no interest in trying to make the farm a paying concern. If her father had not been able to do it with all his expertise, she did not see how she could. And, while she had grown to quite like the man whom Leanne had so unceremoniously dumped, the twenty-nine-year-old male might well be glad to see the back of anyone who bore the Hawkins name.

She had no idea if she was entitled to claim the tenancy, but if not, Ash would be quite within his rights to instigate having her thrown out.

Not wanting the indignity of that, Phinn wondered where on earth she could go. For herself she did not care very much where she went, but it was Ruby she had to think about.

To that end, Phinn took a walk down to the local riding school, run by Peggy Edmonds. And it turned out that going to see Peggy was the best thing she could have done. Because not only was Peggy able to house Ruby, she was even—unbelievably— able to offer Phinn a job. True, it wasn't much of a job, but with a place for Ruby assured, Phinn would have accepted anything.

Apparently Peggy was having a hard time battling with arthritis, and for over a year had been trying to find a buyer for what was now more of a stables than a riding school. But it seemed no one was remotely interested in making her an offer. With her arthritis so bad some days that it was all she could do to get out of bed, if Phinn would like to work as a stable hand, although Peggy could not pay very much, there was a small stall Ruby could have, and she could spend her days in the field with the other horses. As a bonus, there was a tiny flat above one of the stables doing nothing.

It was a furnished flat, with no room for farmhouse furniture, and having been advised by the house clearers that she would have to pay *them* to empty the farmhouse, Phinn got her father's old friend Mickie Yates—an educated, eccentric but loveable jack-of-all-trades—to take everything away for her. It grieved her to see her father's piano go, but there was no space in the tiny flat for it.

So it was as January drew to a close that Phinn walked Ruby down to her new home and then, cutting through the spinney on Broadlands that she knew so well, Phinn took the key to the farmhouse up to the Hall.

Ash Allardyce was not in. Phinn was quite glad about that. After the way her cousin had treated him, dropping him cold like that, it might have been a touch embarrassing.

'I was very sorry to hear about your father, Phinn,' Mrs Starkey said, taking the keys from her.

'Thank you, Mrs Starkey,' Phinn replied quietly, and returned to the stables.

But almost immediately, barely having congratulated herself on how well everything was turning out—she had a job and Ruby was housed and fed—the sky started to fall in.

By late March it crash-landed.

Ruby—probably because of her previous ill-treatment—had always been timid, and needed peace and quiet, but was being bullied by the other much younger horses. Phinn took her on walks away from them as often as she could, but with her own work to do that was not as often as she would have liked.

Then, against all odds, Peggy found a buyer. A buyer who wanted to take possession as soon as it could possibly be achieved.

'I'll talk to her and see if there's any chance of her keeping you on,' Peggy said quickly, on seeing the look of concern on Phinn's face.

Phinn had met Geraldine Walton, a dark-haired woman of around thirty, who was not dissimilar to her cousin in appearance. She had met her on one of Geraldine's 'look around' visits, and had thought she seemed to have a bit of a hard edge to her—which made Phinn not too hopeful.

She was right not to be too hopeful, she soon discovered, for not only was there no job for her, neither was there a place for Ruby. And, not only that, Geraldine Walton was bringing her own staff and requested that Phinn kindly vacate the flat over the stable. As quickly as possible, please.

Now, Phinn, with the late-April sun streaming through the window, looked round the stable flat and knew she had better think about packing up her belongings. Not that she had so very much to pack, but… Her eyes came to rest on the camera her mother, who had visited her last Sunday, had given her to return to Ash on Leanne's behalf.

Feeling a touch guilty that her mother's visit had been a couple of days ago now and she had done nothing about it, Phinn went and picked up the piece of photographic equipment. No time like the present—and she could get Ruby away from the other horses for a short while.

Collecting Ruby, Phinn walked her across the road and took the shortcut through the spinney. In no time she was approaching the impressive building that was Broadlands Hall.

Leanne Hawkins was not her favourite cousin just then.

She had been unkind to Ash Allardyce, and, while Phinn considered that had little to do with her, she would much prefer that her cousin did her own dirty work. It seemed that her mother, who had no illusions about Leanne, had doubted that Ash would have got his expensive camera back at all were it not for the fact that he, still very much smitten, used it as an excuse to constantly telephone Leanne. Apparently Leanne could not be bothered to talk to him, and had asked Phinn to make sure he had his rotten camera back.

Phinn neared the Hall, hoping that it would again be Mrs Starkey who answered her ring at the door. Cowardly it might be, but she had no idea what she could say to Ash Allardyce. While she might be annoyed with Leanne, Leanne was still family, and family loyalty said that she could not say how shabbily she personally felt Leanne had treated him.

Phinn pulled the bell-tug, half realising that if Ash was still as smitten with Leanne as he had been, he was unlikely to say anything against her cousin that might provoke her having to stand up for her. She…

Phinn's thoughts evaporated as she heard the sound of someone approaching the stout oak door from within. Camera in one hand, Ruby's rein in the other, Phinn prepared to smile.

Then the front door opened and was pulled back—and her smile never made it. For it was not Mrs Starkey who stood there, and neither was it Ash Allardyce. Ash was fair-haired, but this man had ink-black hair—and an expression that was far from welcoming! He was tall, somewhere in his mid-thirties—and clearly not pleased to see her. She knew very well who he was—strangely, she had never forgotten his face. His good-looking face.

But his grim expression didn't let up when in one dark glance he took in the slender, delphinium-blue-eyed woman with a thick strawberry-blonde plait hanging over one shoulder, a camera in one hand and a rein in the other.

All too obviously he had recognised the camera, because his grim expression became grimmer if anything.

'And you are?' he demanded without preamble.

Yes, she, although having never been introduced to him, knew very well this was the man who was ultimately responsible for her father receiving that notice to quit. To quit the land that his family had farmed for generations. It passed her by just then that her father had done very little to keep the farm anything like the farm it had been for those generations.

'I'm Phinn Hawkins,' she replied—a touch belligerently it had to be admitted. 'I've—'

His eyes narrowed at her tone, though his tone was none too sweet either as he challenged shortly, 'What do you want on my land, Hawkins?'

And that made her mad. 'And you are?' she demanded, equally as sharp as he.

She was then forced to bear his tough scrutiny for several uncompromising seconds as he studied her. But, just when she was beginning to think she would have to run for his name, 'Tyrell Allardyce,' he supplied at last. And, plainly unused to repeating himself, 'What do you want?' he barked.

'Nothing you can supply, Allardyce!' she tossed back at him, refusing to be intimidated. Stretching out a hand, she offered the camera. 'Give this to your brother,' she ordered loftily. But at her mention of his brother, she was made to endure a look that should have turned her to stone.

'Get off my land!' he gritted between clenched teeth. 'And—' his tone was threatening '—don't *ever* set foot on it again!'

His look was so malevolent it took everything she had to keep from flinching. 'Huh!' she scorned, and, badly wanting to run as fast as she could away from this man and his menacing look, she turned Ruby about and ambled away from the Hall.

By the time she and Ruby had entered the spinney, some

of Phinn's equilibrium had started to return. And a short while later she was starting to be thoroughly cross with herself that she had just walked away without acquainting him with a few of the do's and don'ts of living in the country.

Who did he think he was, for goodness' sake? She had *always* roamed the estate lands freely. True, there were certain areas she knew she was not supposed to trespass over. But she had been brought up using the Broadlands fields and acres as her right of way! She was darn sure she wasn't going to alter that now!

The best thing Ty Allardyce could do, she fumed, would be to take himself and his big city ways back to London. And stay there! And good riddance to him too! She had now met him, but she hoped she never had the misfortune of seeing his forbidding, disagreeable face ever again!

CHAPTER TWO

SOMEHOW, in between worrying about finding a new home for herself and Ruby, Phinn could not stop thoughts of Ty Allardyce from intruding. Though, as the days went by and the weekend passed and another week began, Phinn considered that to have the man so much in and out of her mind was not so surprising. How *dared* he order her off his land?

Well, tough on him! It was a lovely early May day—what could be nicer than to take Ruby and go for a walk? Leaving the flat, Phinn went down to collect her. But, before she could do more than put a halter on the mare, Geraldine Walton appeared from nowhere to waylay her. Phinn knew what was coming before Geraldine so much as opened her mouth. She was not mistaken.

'I'm sorry to have to be blunt, Phinn,' Geraldine began, 'but I really do need the stable flat by the end of the week.'

'I'm working on it,' Phinn replied, at her wits' end. She had phoned round everywhere she could think of, but nobody wanted her *and* Ruby. And Ruby fretted if she was away from her for very long, so no way was Ruby going anywhere without her. Phinn had wondered about them both finding some kind of animal sanctuary, willing to take them both, but then again, having recently discovered that Ruby was unhappy with other horses around, she did not want to give her ailing

mare more stress. 'Leave it with me,' she requested, and a few
minutes later crossed the road on to Broadlands property and
walked Ruby through the spinney, feeling all churned up at
how it would break her heart—and Ruby's—to have to leave
her anywhere.

The majestic Broadlands Hall was occasionally visible
through gaps in the trees in the small wood, but Phinn was
certain that Ty Allardyce would by now be back in London,
beavering away at whatever it was financiers beavered away
at. Though just in case, as they walked through fields that
bordered the adjacent grounds and gardens they had always
walked through—or in earlier days ridden through—she made
sure that she and Ruby were well out of sight, should anyone
at the Hall be looking out.

Hoping not to meet him, if London's loss was Bishops
Thornby's gain and he *was* still around, Phinn moved on, and
was taking a stroll near the pool where she and her father had
so often swum when she did bump into an Allardyce. It was Ash.

It would have been quite natural for Phinn to pause, say
hello, make some sort of polite conversation. But she was so
shaken by the change in the man from the last time she had
seen him that she barely recognised him, and all words went
from her. Ash looked terrible!

'Hello, Ash,' she did manage, but was unwilling to move
on. He looked positively ill, and she searched for something
else to say. 'Did you get your camera all right?' she asked, and
could have bitten out her tongue. Was her cousin responsible
in any way for this dreadful change in him? Surely not? Ash
looked grey, sunken-eyed, and at least twenty pounds lighter!

'Yes, thanks,' he replied, no smile, his eyes dull and
lifeless. But, brightening up a trifle, 'Have you seen Leanne
recently?' he asked.

Fleetingly she wondered if Ash, so much in love with
Leanne, might have found cause to suspect she was money-

minded and, not wanting to lose her, not told her that it was his brother who owned Broadlands. But she had not seen her cousin since the day Leanne had learned that Ash was not the one with the money and had so callously dropped him.

'Leanne—er—doesn't come this way—er—now,' Phinn answered, feeling awkward, her heart aching for this man who seemed bereft that his love wanted nothing more to do with him.

'I don't suppose she has anywhere to stay now that you're no longer at Honeysuckle Farm,' he commented, and as he began to stroll along with her, Phinn did not feel able to tell him that the only time Leanne had ever shown an interest in staying any length of time at the farm had been when she'd had her sights set on being mistress of Broadlands Hall. 'I'm sorry that you had to leave, by the way,' Ash stated.

And her heart went out to this gaunt man whose clothes were just about hanging on him. 'I couldn't have stayed,' she replied, and, hoping to lighten his mood, 'I don't think I'd make a very good farmer.' Not sure which was best for him—to talk of Leanne or not to talk of Leanne—she opted to enquire, 'Have you found a new tenant for Honeysuckle yet?'

'I'm—undecided what to do,' Ash answered, and suddenly the brilliant idea came to Phinn that, if he had not yet got a tenant for the farm, maybe she and Ruby could go back and squat there for a while; the weather was so improved and it was quite warm for early summer. Ruby would be all right there. But Ash was going on. 'I did think I might take it over myself, but I don't seem able to—er—make decisions on anything just at the moment.'

Ash's confession took the squatting idea from Phinn momentarily. Leanne again! How *could* she have been so careless of this sensitive man's fine feelings?

'I'm sure you and Honeysuckle would be good for each other—if that's what you decide to do,' Phinn replied gently.

And Ash gave a shaky sigh, as if he had wandered off for

a moment. 'I think I'd like to work outdoors. Better than an
indoor job anyway.' And, with a self-deprecating look, 'I tried
a career in the big business world.'

'You didn't like it?'

He shook his head. 'I don't think I'm the academic type.
That's more Ty's forte. He's the genius in the family when it
comes to the cut and thrust of anything like that.' Ash seemed
to wander off again for a moment or two, and then, like the
caring kind of person he was, he collected himself to enquire,
'You're settled in your new accommodation, Phinn?'

'Well—er…' Phinn hesitated. It was unthinkable that she
should burden him with her problems, but the idea of squatting back at Honeysuckle was picking at her again.

'You're not settled?' Ash took up.

'Geraldine—she's the new owner of the stables—wants to
do more on the riding school front, and needs my flat for a
member of her staff,' Phinn began.

'But you work there too?'

'Well, no, actually. Er…'

'You're out of a job *and* a home?' Ash caught on.

'Ruby and I have until the end of this week,' Phinn said
lightly, and might well have put in a pitch for his permission
to use Honeysuckle as a stop-gap measure—only she chanced
to look across to him, and once more into his dull eyes, and
she simply did not have the heart. He appeared to have the
weight of the world on his shoulders, and she just could not
add to his burden.

'Ruby?' he asked. 'I didn't know you had a child?'

He looked so concerned that Phinn rushed in to reassure him.
'I don't.' She patted Ruby's shoulder. 'This lovely girl is Ruby.'

His look of concern changed to one of relief. 'I don't know
much about horses, but…'

Phinn smiled. There wasn't a better-groomed horse anywhere, but there was no mistaking Ruby's years. 'She's

getting on a bit now, and her health isn't so good, but—' She broke off when, turning to glance at Ruby, she saw a male figure in the distance, coming their way at a fast pace. Uh-oh! Ash hadn't seen him, but she didn't fancy a row with Ty Allardyce in front of him. 'That reminds me—we'd better be off. It's time for Ruby's medication,' she said. 'Nice to see you again, Ash. Bye.'

And with that, unfortunately having to go towards the man she was starting to think of as 'that dastardly Ty Allardyce', she led Ruby away.

'Bye, Phinn,' Ash bade her, seeing nothing wrong with her abrupt departure as he went walking on in the opposite direction.

With Ruby not inclined to hurry, there was no way Phinn could avoid the owner of the Hall, who also happened to be the owner of the land she was trespassing on. They were on a collision course!

Several remarks entered her head before Ty Allardyce was within speaking distance. Though when he was but a few yards from her—and looking tough with it—her voice nearly failed her. But in her view she had done nothing wrong.

'Not back in London yet, I see!' she remarked, more coolly than she felt.

'Why, you—' Ty Allardyce began angrily, but checked his anger, to demand, 'What have you been saying to my brother?'

While part of Phinn recognised that his question had come from concern for Ash, she did not like Ty Allardyce and never would. 'What's it got to do with you?' she challenged loftily.

His dark grey eyes glinted, and she would not have been all that surprised had she felt his hands around her throat—he looked quite prepared to attempt to throttle her! 'It has everything to do with me,' he controlled his ire to inform her shortly. 'You Hawkins women don't give a damn who you hurt…'

'Hawkins women!' she exclaimed, starting to get angry herself. 'What the devil do you mean by that?'

'Your reputation precedes you!'

'Reputation?'

'Your father was devastated when your mother dumped him. My—'

Mother *dumped* him! Phinn was on the instant furious, but somehow managed to control her feeling of wanting to throttle *him* to butt in with mock sarcasm. 'Oh, really, Allardyce. You truly must try to stop listening to village gossip…'

'You're saying he *wasn't* devastated? That his reason for not paying the rent had nothing at all to do with the fact that your mother took up with some other man and left your father a total wreck?'

Oh, Lord. That quickly squashed her anger. She did not doubt that her father *had* been capable of conveying his marriage break-up as his reason without exactly saying so. But his marriage break-up had had nothing to do with him not paying the rent—the fact the rent had not been paid had been more to do with her mother's hands no longer being on the purse strings. It was true, Phinn had discovered, that the rent had only ceased to be paid when her mother had left.

'What went on between my father and mother is nothing at all to do with you!' Phinn stated coldly, wanting her anger back. 'It's none of your business…'

'When it comes to my brother I'll make it my business. You've seen him! You've seen how gutted he is that your cousin ditched him the same way your mother ditched your father. I'm not having another Hawkins anywhere near him. Get off my land and stay off it! And,' he went on icily when she opened her mouth, 'don't give me "Huh!" This is your last warning. If I catch you trespassing again I'll have you in court before you can blink!'

'Have you quite finished?'

'I hope never to have to speak to you again,' he confirmed. 'You just leave my brother alone.'

'Be glad to!' she snapped, her eyes darkening. 'I don't know what Bishops Thornby ever did to deserve the likes of you, but for my money it was the worst day's work he ever did when old Mr Caldicott sold this estate to you!' Thereafter ignoring him, she addressed the mare. 'Come on, Rubes. You're much too sweet to have to stand and listen to this loathsome man!'

With that, she put her nose in the air and sauntered off. Unfortunately, because of Ruby's slow gait, she was prevented from marching off as she would have wished. She hoped the dastardly Allardyce got the idea anyway.

Her adrenalin was still pumping when she took Ruby back to her stall. Honestly, that man!

Phinn wasted no time the next day. Once she had attended to all Ruby's needs, she made the long walk up to Honeysuckle Farm. She walked into the familiar farmyard, but, having been away from the farm for around three months, as she stood and stared about she was able to see it for the first time from a different perspective. She had to admit to feeling a little shaken.

Rusting pieces of machinery littered the yard, and there was a general air of neglect everywhere. Which there would be, she defended her father. Had he lived he would have repaired and sold on the rusting and clapped out pieces. Had he lived...

Avoiding thoughts that some of the machinery had lain there rusting for years, and not just since last October when her father had died, and the fact that the place had become to be more and more run-down over the years but that until today she had never noticed it, Phinn went to take a look at the old barn that had used to be Ruby's home.

The secure door latch had broken years ago, but, as her father had so laughingly said, they had nothing worth stealing so why bother repairing it? That his logic was a touch different from most people's had all been part of the man she had adored. It hadn't been that he was idle, he'd just thought on a different and more pleasurable level.

The barn smelt musty, and not too pleasant. But it was a sunny day, so Phinn propped the doors open wide and went in. Everything about the place screamed, *no!* But what alternative did she have? Ruby, her timid darling Ruby, would by far prefer to be up here in the old barn than where she was. Had Phinn had any idea of Ruby's fear of the other horses she would never have taken her there in the first place. Too late now to be wise after the event!

Looking for plus points, Phinn knew that Ruby would be better on her own, away from the younger horses. As well as being timid, Ruby was a highly sensitive mare, and with their mutual attachment to each other, Honeysuckle was the best place for them. Another plus: it was dry—mainly. And there was a field. Several, in fact. Overgrown with weeds and clutter, but in Phinn's view it wouldn't take her long to clear it and put up some sort of temporary fencing.

With matters pertaining to Ruby sorted out in her head, Phinn crossed the yard, found a ladder, and was able to gain entry into the farmhouse by climbing up to a bedroom window. Forcing the window did not take a great deal of effort, and once in she went through to what had once been her own bedroom.

It smelt musty, but then it hadn't been used in months. There was no electricity, so she would have to do without heat or light, but looking on the brighter side she felt sure that Mickie Yates would cart her few belongings up for her. Mickie had been a good friend of her father's, and she knew she could rely on him not to tell anyone that she was squatting—trespassing, Allardyce would call it if he knew—at Honeysuckle.

Phinn left Honeysuckle Farm endeavouring not to think what her mother's reaction to her plan would be. Appalled would not cover it.

By Thursday of that week Phinn was trying to tell herself that she felt quite enthusiastic about her proposed move. She had been to see Mickie Yates and found him in his workshop, up to his elbows in muck and grease, but with the loveliest smile of welcome on his face for her.

Whatever he thought when she asked for use of him and one of his vehicles to transport her cases and horse equipment on Friday she did not know. All he'd said was, 'After three suit you, Phinn?'

She knew he would be having his 'lunch' in the Cat and Drum until two fifty-five. 'Lovely thank you, Mickie,' she had replied.

It was a surprisingly hot afternoon, and Phinn, not certain when she would be in the village again, decided to walk Ruby to the village farrier. It would be even hotter at the forge, so she changed out of her more usual jeans and top, exchanging them for a thin, loose-fitting sleeveless cotton dress. Donning some sandals, she felt certain that by now grumpy Allardyce *must* be back in London, where he surely more particularly belonged.

Perhaps after their visit to Idris Owen, the farrier and blacksmith, a man who could turn his hand to anything and who had been another friend of her father's, Phinn and Ruby might take another stroll in the shady spinney.

Knowing that she should be packing her belongings prior to tomorrow's move, she left her flat— and on the way out bumped into Geraldine Walton. Geraldine seemed difficult to miss these days. But for once Phinn was not anxious about meeting her.

'You do know I shall want the flat on Saturday?' Geraldine began a touch stiffly, before Phinn could say a word.

'You shall have it,' she replied. 'Ruby and I are moving tomorrow.'

Geraldine's severe look lightened. 'You are? Oh, good! Er…I hope you've found somewhere—suitable?'

Phinn ignored the question in her voice. Villages being villages, she knew she could not hope to keep her new address secret for very long. But, her new address being part of the Broadlands Estate, the longer it was kept from Ty Allardyce the better. Not that she was aware if Geraldine even knew him, but there was no point in inviting more of his wrath—and a *definite* court summons—if they were acquainted.

'Most suitable,' she replied with a smile, and, aiming to make the best of what life was currently throwing at her, she went to collect Ruby.

Idris greeted Phinn with the same warm smile she had received from Mickie Yates. Idris was somewhere around fifty, a huge mountain of a man, with a heart as big. 'How's my best girl?' he asked, as he always did. No matter what time of day she visited, he always seemed to have a pint of beer on the go. 'Help yourself,' he offered, as he checked Ruby's hooves and shoes.

Phinn still did not like beer any better than she had when she had first tasted it. But it was blisteringly hot in there, and to take a healthy swig of his beer—as encouraged so to do in the past by her father—was now traditional. She picked up the pot and drank to her father's memory.

When he was done, Idris told her that she owed him nothing, and she knew he would be upset if she insisted on paying him. So, thanking him, she and Ruby left the smithy and headed for the small wood.

Keeping a watchful eye out for the elder Allardyce, Phinn chatted quietly to Ruby all the way through the spinney, and Ruby, having a good day for once, talked back, nodded and generally kept close.

Once out of the shaded spinney, they strolled towards the pool with the heat starting to beat down on them. Ruby loved the warmth, and Phinn, catching a glimpse of the pool, had started to think in terms of what a wonderful day for a swim.

No, I shouldn't. She attempted to ignore that part of her that was seeing no earthly reason why she shouldn't take a quick dip. She glanced about—no one in sight. They ambled on, reaching the pool and some more trees, and all the while Phinn fought down the demon temptation.

She would never know whether or not she would have given in to that demon had not something happened just then that drove all other thoughts from her head. Suddenly in the stillness she heard a yell of alarm. It came from the dark side of the pool. It was the cry of someone in trouble!

In moments she had run down the bank and did not have to search very far to see who was in trouble—and what the trouble was! Oh, God! Her blood ran cold. Across from the shallow end was a dark area called the Dark Pool—because that was precisely what it was: dark. Dark because it was overhung with trees and the sun never got to it. Not only was it dark, it was deep, and it was icy. And everyone knew that you must *never* attempt to swim there. Only someone *was* in there! Ash Allardyce! He was flailing about and quite clearly close to drowning!

All Phinn knew then was that she had to get to him quickly. There was a small bridge spanning the narrow part of the pool, but that was much farther down. And time was of the essence. There was no time to think, only time to act. Her father had taught her lifesaving, and had taught her well. Up until then it was a skill she had never needed to use.

Even as these thoughts were flashing thought her mind Phinn was kicking off her sandals and pulling her dress over her head. Knowing she had to get to Ash, and fast, and all before she could query the wisdom of what she was doing, Phinn was running for the water and taking a racing dive straight in.

After having been so hot, the water felt icy, but there was no time to think about that now. Only time to get to Ash. Executing a sprinting crawl, Phinn reached him in no time flat, gasped a warning, 'Stay still or you'll kill us both,' turned him onto his back and, glad for the moment that he was twenty pounds lighter than he had been, towed him to the nearest bank, which was now on the opposite side from where she had first seen him.

How long he had been struggling she had no idea. 'Cramp!' he managed to gasp, and managed to sit up, head down, his arms on his knees, exhausted, totally drained of energy.

It had all happened so quickly, but now that it was over Phinn felt pretty drained herself, and had an idea she knew pretty much how a mother must feel when she had just found her lost child. 'You should have had more sense,' she berated him with what breath she could find. 'Everybody *knows* you don't swim in *that* part of the pool.' Suddenly she was feeling inexplicably weepy. Shock, she supposed. Then she remembered Ruby, and looked to the other bank. She could not see her. 'I'll be back,' she said, and took off.

Not to swim this time—she didn't feel like going back in there in a hurry—but to run down to the small bridge. It fleetingly crossed her mind as she ran to wonder if Ash had perhaps been a touch suicidal to have chosen to swim where he had. Then she recalled he had said he'd had a cramp, and she began to feel better about leaving him. She had been brought up *knowing* that a deep shelf had been excavated on that side of the pool for some reason that was now lost in the mists of time. The water was deep there—nobody knew how deep, but so deep as to never heat up, and was regarded locally with the greatest respect. Ash, who hadn't been brought up in the area, could not possibly have known unless someone had told him. Well, he knew now!

Phinn ran across the bridge, and as she did so she saw with

relief that Ruby had not wandered off and that she was quite safe. Phinn's relief was short-lived, however, because in that same glance she saw none other than Ty Allardyce. Phinn came to an abrupt halt.

Oh, help! He was facing away from her and had not yet spotted her. He was looking about—perhaps searching for his brother? He was close to Ruby. Then Phinn saw that he was not only close to Ruby, he had hold of her rein. Phinn knew then that it was not his brother he was searching for but Ruby's owner—and that Ruby's owner was in deep trouble!

As if aware of someone behind him, Ty Allardyce turned round. Turned and, as if he could not believe his eyes, stared at her.

And that was when Phinn became aware of how she was dressed—or rather *undressed*. A quick glance down proved that she was as good as naked! Standing there in her wet underwear she was conscious that her waterlogged bra and briefs were now transparent, the pink tips of her breasts hardened and clearly visible to the man staring at her.

Her face glowed a fiery red. 'A gentleman would turn his back,' she hissed, with what voice she could find.

Ty Allardyce favoured her with a hard stare, but was in no hurry to turn around. 'So he would—for a lady,' he drawled.

Phinn wanted to hit him, but she wasn't going any closer. And he, surveying her from her soggy braided hair down to the tip of her bare toes, took his time, his insolent gaze moving back up her long, long shapely legs, thighs and belly. By this time her arms were crossed in front of her body. Strangely, it was only when his glance rested on her fiercely blushing face that he gave her the benefit of the term 'lady' and, while still holding Ruby's rein, turned his back on her.

In next to no time Phinn had retrieved her dress and sandals and, having been careless how her dress had landed, found that her hands were shaking when she went to turn it right side out.

But once she had her dress over her shoulders, she felt her former spirit returning. She had to go close up to him to take Ruby's rein, and, as embarrassed as she felt, she somehow managed to find an impudent, 'Lovely day for a dip!'

His reply was to turn and favour her with one of his hard stares. It seemed to her as if he was deciding whether or not to pick her up and throw her in for another dip.

Attempting to appear casual, she moved to the other side of Ruby. Not a moment too soon, she realised, as, not caring for her insolence, 'That's it!' he rapped, his eyes angry on her by now much paler face. 'I've warned you twice. You'll receive notice from my lawyers in the morning.'

'You have my address?' she enquired nicely—and felt inclined to offer him her new address; but at his hard-eyed expression she thought better of it.

Ty Allardyce drew one very harsh, long-suffering breath. 'Enough!' he snarled. 'If you're not on your way inside the next ten seconds, I shall personally be escorting you and that flea-bitten old nag off my land!'

'Flea-bitten!' she gasped. How *dared* he?

'Now!' he threatened, making a move to take Ruby's rein from her.

'Leave her alone!' Phinn threatened back, her tone murderous as she knocked his hand away. She was not sure yet that she wasn't going to hit him—he was well and truly asking for it! Emotional tears sprang to her eyes.

Tears he spotted, regardless that she'd managed to hold them back and prevent them from falling. 'Of for G—' he began impatiently. And, as if more impatient with himself than with her, because her shining eyes had had more effect on him than her murderous threat, 'Clear off, stay off—and leave my brother alone!'

Only then did Phinn remember Ash. A quick glance to the other side of the pool showed he had recovered and was getting to his feet, which told her she could safely leave him. 'Wouldn't touch either of you with a bargepole,' she told Ty loftily, and turned Ruby about and headed in the direction of the spinney.

With everything that had taken place playing back in her mind, Phinn walked on with Ruby. She had no idea how long it was since she had seen Ash in trouble—ten perhaps fifteen minutes? A glance to her watch showed that it did not care much for underwater activity and would never be the same again.

She felt ashamed that she had very nearly cried in front of that brute. *Flea-bitten old nag!* But she started to accept—now that she was away from him, away from the pool—that perhaps she had started to feel a bit of reaction after first seeing Ash in difficulties, taking a header in to get him out, and then, to top it all, being confronted by Ty Allardyce.

Yes, it must be shock, she realised. There was no other explanation for her thinking, as she had at the time, that Ty Allardyce had been sensitive to a woman's tears.

Sensitive! She must be in shock still! That insensitive brute didn't have a sensitive bone in his body! How could he have? He had actually called her darling Rubes a flea-bitten old nag! Oh, how she wished she had hit him.

Well, one thing was for sure. She would take great delight in marking any lawyer's letter that arrived for her tomorrow 'address unknown', before she happily popped it in the post box to be sent speedily straight back whence it came!

CHAPTER THREE

As SOON as she had settled Ruby, Phinn went to the stable flat, stripped off, showered and washed the pool out of her hair. Donning fresh underwear, a pair of shorts and a tee shirt, she wrapped a towel around her hair and made herself a cup of tea. She admitted that she was still feeling a little shaken up by the afternoon's events.

Although, on reflection, she wasn't sure which had disturbed her the most: the unexpectedness of coming upon Ash Allardyce without warning and her efforts to get the drowning man to the bank, or the fact that his hard-nosed brother had so insolently stood there surveying her when she had stood as near to naked as if it made no difference.

He quite obviously thought she had taken advantage of the hot weather to strip off to her underwear and have a swim in waters that belonged to his lands. And he hadn't liked that, had he? He with his, 'Clear off, stay off—and leave my brother alone!'

She cared not whether Ash ever told him the true facts of her swim. She had always swum there—weather permitting. Though she did recall one marvellously hysterical time when it had come on to rain while she and her father had been swimming, and he had declared that since they couldn't get any wetter they might as well carry on swimming.

Barefooted, she padded to get another towel and, because her long hair took for ever to dry naturally, she towelled it as dry as she could, brushed it out, and left her hair hanging down over her shoulders to dry when it would.

Meantime, she packed her clothes and placed a couple of suitcases near the door, ready for when Mickie Yates would come round at three tomorrow afternoon. Now she had better start packing away her china, and the few ornaments and mementoes she had been unable to part with from her old home.

The mantelpiece was bare, and she had just finished clearing the shelves, when someone came knocking at her door. Geraldine coming to check that she was truly leaving tomorrow, Phinn supposed, padding to the door. She pulled it open—only to receive another shock!

Finding herself staring up into the cool grey eyes of Ty Allardyce, Phinn was for the moment struck dumb. And as he stared into her darkening blue eyes, he seemed in no hurry to start a conversation either.

The fact that she was now dry, and clad in shorts and top, as opposed to dripping and in her underwear as the last time he had studied her, made Phinn feel no better. She saw his glance flick to her long strawberry-blonde hair, free from its plait, and pulled herself sharply together.

'As I live and breathe—the lesser-spotted superior Allardyce,' she waded in. 'Now who's trespassing?'

To his credit, he took her remark equably. 'I should like to talk to you,' he said for openers.

'Tough! Get off my—er...' *damn* '...doorstep.'

His answer to her command was to ignore it. And, much to her annoyance, he did no more than push his way into what had been her sitting room-cum-kitchen.

'You're leaving tomorrow?' he suggested, his eyes moving from her suitcases to the boxes of packed teacups, plates and ornaments.

Phinn fought to find some sharp comeback, but couldn't find one. 'Yes,' she replied, belligerent because she saw no reason to be any other way with this man who wanted to curtail her right to use and respect his grounds as her own.

'Where are you going?' he enquired, and she hated it that, when she could never remember any man making her blush before, this man seemed to be able to do so without the smallest effort.

'I—er…' she mumbled, and turned away from him, walking towards the window in a vain hope that he had not noticed she had gone red.

'You're looking guilty about something,' he commented, closing the door and coming further into the room, adding, as she turned to face him, 'I do hope, Miss Hawkins, that I'm not going to wake up on Saturday morning and find you camping out on my front lawn?'

The idea amused her, and despite herself her lips twitched. And she supposed that 'Miss Hawkins' was one better than the plain 'Hawkins' he had used before. But she quickly stamped down on what she considered must be a quirk in her sense of humour. 'To be honest, that was something I hadn't thought of doing,' she replied.

'But?'

This man was as sharp as a tack! He knew full well that there was a 'but'. 'But nothing,' she replied stiffly. She didn't want a spanner thrown into the works of her arrangements at this late stage. But Ty Allardyce continued to look back at her, his mind fully at work, she didn't doubt. 'Well, I've things to do. Thank you for popping by,' she said coolly, moving towards the door, knowing full well that this wasn't a social call, but at a loss to know what else one would call it.

'What you would need,' he stated thoughtfully, his glance lighting briefly on her long length of leg in the short shorts, 'is somewhere you can lay your head, and somewhere where at the same time you can stable that—'

'Her name is Ruby,' Phinn cut in, starting to bridle. 'The flea-bitten old nag, as you so delightfully called her, is Ruby.'

'I apologise,' he replied, and that surprised her so much she could only stand there and blink. And blink again when he went on. 'Do you know, I really don't think I can allow you to go back to Honeysuckle Farm? It—'

'How did you know I intended to go there?' she gasped in amazement. Surely Mickie hadn't…?

He hadn't. 'I didn't know. That is I wasn't sure until you just this minute confirmed it.'

'Clever devil!' she sniffed. Then quickly realised that she was in a hole that looked like getting bigger and bigger—if she couldn't do something about it. 'Look,' she said, taking a deep breath, 'I know you're cross with me—full-time, permanently. But I wouldn't harm the place. I'd—'

'Out of the question,' he cut in forthrightly.

'Why?' she demanded, when common sense told her she was going about this in totally the wrong way.

'There aren't any services up there for a start.'

'I won't need any. I've got a supply of candles. And it's too warm for me to need heating. And…'

'And what if it rains and the roof leaks?'

'It doesn't. I was up there the other…' Oh, grief—just think before you speak!

'You've been inside?' he demanded. 'You still have a key?'

'Yes and no.' He looked impatient. She hated him. 'Yes, I've been inside. And, no, I haven't got a key.'

'You got in—how?'

It wouldn't have taken much for her to tell him to get lost, but she was still hopeful of moving back to Honeysuckle Farm tomorrow. 'I—um—got in through one of the bedroom windows,' she confessed.

'You climbed in...' He shook his head slightly, as if hardly believing this female. 'You include breaking and entering in your list of skills?'

'I'm desperate!' she exclaimed shortly. 'Ruby's not well, and—' She broke off. Damn the man. It must still be shock—she was feeling weepy again. She turned her back on him, wanting to order him out, but ready to swallow her pride and plead with him if she had to.

But then, to her astonishment and to her disbelieving ears, she discovered that she did not have to plead with him at all. Because, staggeringly, Ty Allardyce was stating, 'I think we can find you somewhere a bit better than the present condition of Honeysuckle Farm to live.'

Things like that just did not happen for people like Delphinnium Hawkins—well, not lately anyhow. She stared at him open-mouthed. He didn't like her. She definitely didn't like him. So why? 'For Ruby too?' she asked slowly.

'For Ruby too,' he confirmed.

'Where?' she asked, not believing it but desperately wanting to.

'Up at the Hall. You could come and live with—'

'Now, wait a minute!' she cut in bluntly. 'I don't know what you think I am, but let me tell—'

'Oh, for heaven's sake!' He cut her off irritably. Then, taking a steadying breath, let her know that she could not be more wrong. 'While I'll acknowledge you may have the best pair of legs I've seen in a while—and the rest of you isn't so bad either...' She refused to visibly blench, because he must be referring to the sight he'd had of her well-proportioned breasts, pink tips protruding. 'I have better things to do with my free time than want to bed one of the village locals!'

Village locals! Well, that put her in her place. 'You should be so lucky!' she sniffed. But, with Ruby in mind, she could not afford to be offended for very long. 'Why would you want me living up at the Hall?'

'Shall we sit down?' he suggested.

Perhaps her legs would be less on display if she sat down. Phinn moved to one chair and he went and occupied the other one. Then, waiting until she looked ready to listen, he began, 'You did me a service today that will render me forever in your debt.'

'Oh, I wouldn't say that.' She shrugged off his comment, but realised then that he now knew all about his brother's attack of cramp. 'See where trespassing will get you!'

'Had you not trespassed…had you not been there—' He broke off. 'It doesn't bear thinking about,' he said, his jaw clenching as if he was getting on top of some emotion.

'Ash wasn't to know that that part of the pool is treacherous. That you have to stick strictly to the shallows if you want to swim,' she attempted lightly.

But Ty was not making light of it, and seemed to know precisely how tragic the consequences could have been. 'But you knew it. And even so—according to Ash when he was able to reflect back—you did the finest and fastest running racing dive he'd ever seen. He said that you dived straight in, not a moment's hesitation, to get him out.'

'Had you arrived a little earlier than you did, I'd have happily let *you* go in,' she murmured, starting to feel a touch embarrassed. With relief she saw, unexpectedly, the way Ty's mouth had picked up at the corners and knew her attempt at humour—her intimation that she would quite happily have let him take his chances on drowning—had reached his own sense of humour.

Though he was not to be drawn away from the seriousness of their discussion it seemed, because he continued. 'You saved my brother's life with not a thought for your own, when you knew full well about that treacherous side of the pool. You went straight in.'

'I did stop to kick my sandals off and yank my dress over my head,' she reminded him, again attempting to make light of it.

But then wished that she hadn't, when grey eyes looked straight into hers and he commented, 'I have not forgotten,' adding in a low murmur, 'I doubt I ever shall. I thought you'd been skinny-dipping at first.' He brought himself up short. 'Anyhow, Ash—for all he's lost a lot of weight—is still quite heavy. Had he struggled, you could both have drowned. Dear God—' He broke off again, swallowing down his anguish.

Seeing his mental torment, and even if she didn't like him, Phinn just had to tell him, 'Ash didn't struggle. It wasn't an attempt at suicide, if that's what you think. It was cramp, pure and simple. The water's icy there. There's a deep shelf... He...'

Ty Allardyce smiled then. It was the first smile he had ever directed at her and her heart went thump. He was *so* handsome! 'I know he wasn't attempting to take his own life,' he agreed. 'But from that remark it's obvious that you've observed that my brother is...extremely vulnerable at the moment.'

Phinn nodded. Yes, she knew that. 'I know you blame me in part, but truthfully there was nothing I could have done to stop it. I mean, I didn't know that Leanne would—er—break it off with him the way she did.'

'Perhaps I was unfair to blame you,' Ty conceded. 'But to get to other matters—Ash tells me you have a problem, with no job and no home for you and your—Ruby. I,' he stated, 'am in a position to offer you both.'

A home *and* a job? Things like this just did *not* happen. 'I don't want your charity!' she erupted.

'My God, you're touchy!' Ty bit back. But then, looking keenly at her, 'You're not...? Are you in shock? Starting to suffer after-effects from what happened today?'

Phinn rather thought she might be. And—oh, grief—she was feeling weepy again. 'Look, can you go back to being nasty again? I can cope with you better when you're being a brute!'

He wasn't offended, but nor was he reverting to being the brute that always put her on her mettle. 'Have you any family near?' he asked, quite kindly.

This—his niceness—was unnerving. So unnerving that she found she was actually telling him. 'My mother lives in Gloucester, but…'

'I'll drive you there,' he decided. 'Get—'

'I'm not—' she started to protest.

'Stop being argumentative,' he ordered. 'You're in no condition to drive.' And, when she would have protested further, 'You'll probably get the shakes any minute now,' he went on. 'It will be safer all round if I'm at the wheel.'

Honestly—this man! 'Will you stop trying to bulldoze me along?' she flared crossly. 'Yes, I feel a bit shaken,' she admitted. 'But nothing I can't cope with. And I'm not going anywhere.'

'If I can't take you to your mother, I'll take you back to the Hall with me.' He ignored what she had just said.

'No, you won't!' she exploded, going on quickly. 'Apart from anything else, I'm not leaving Ruby. She's—'

'She'll be all right until you pick her up tomorrow,' he countered. 'You can—'

'You can stop right there. Just *stop* it!' she ordered. 'I'm not going anywhere today. And when I do go, Ruby goes with me.'

Ty Allardyce observed the determined look of her. And, plainly a man who did not take defeat lightly, he gave her a stern expression of his own. 'I'll make you some tea,' he said, quite out of nowhere—and she just had to burst out laughing. That just made him stare at her.

'I'm sorry,' she apologized, and, quickly sobering, 'I know tea is said to be good for shock, but I've had some tea and I don't want more. And please,' she went on before he could argue, 'can we just accept that I know you truly appreciate my towing Ash back onto terra firma this afternoon and then forget all about it?'

Steady grey eyes bored into her darkened blue ones. 'You want to go back to me being the brute up at the Hall who keeps trying to turf you off his land?'

Phinn nodded, starting to feel better suddenly. 'And I'll go back to being the—er—village local...' Her lips twitched, and she saw his do the same before they both sobered, and she went on. 'The village local who thinks you've one heck of a nerve daring to stop me from doing things I've always done on Broadlands land.'

He nodded, but informed her, 'You're still not going back to Honeysuckle Farm to live.'

'Oh, come on!' she exclaimed. 'I have to leave here tomorrow. Geraldine wants the flat for a member of her staff, and I've promised I'll move out.'

'That, as I've mentioned, is not a problem. There's a home and a job waiting for you at the Hall.'

'And a home for Ruby too?'

'At the moment the stable is being used for storage, but you can clear it out tomorrow. It's dry in there and—'

'It has water?'

'It has water,' he confirmed.

'You have other horses?' she asked quickly, and, at his questioning look, 'Ruby's a kind of rescue mare. She was badly treated and has a timid nature. Other horses tend to gang up on her.'

'You've no need to worry on that score. Ruby will have an idyllic life. There's a completely fenced-off paddock too that she can use.'

Phinn knew the paddock, if it was the one she was thinking of. As well as being shaded in part by trees, it also had a large open-ended shed a horse could wander into if it became too hot.

All of a sudden Phinn felt weepy again. She would be glad when this shock was over and done with! Oh, it did sound idyllic.

Oh, Ruby, my darling. 'This is a—a permanent job?' she questioned. 'I mean, you're not going to turf me out after a week?'

'It wouldn't be a permanent position,' he replied. Though he added before she could feel too deflated, 'Let's say six months definite, with a review when the six months are up.'

'I'll take it,' she accepted at once, not needing to think about it. She would have six months in which to sort something else out. Trying not to sound too eager, though unable to hold back, she said, 'I'll do it—whatever the job is. I can cook, clean, garden—catalogue your library…'

'With a couple of part-time helpers, Mrs Starkey runs the house and kitchen admirably, and Jimmie Starkey has all the help he needs in the grounds.'

'And you don't need your library catalogued?' she guessed, ready to offer her secretarial skills but suspecting he had a PA in London far more competent than she would be to take care of those matters.

'The job I have for you is very specialised,' Ty Allardyce stated, and before she could tell him that she was a little short in the specialised skills department, he was going on. 'My work in London and overseas has been such that until recently I've been unable to spend very much time down here.'

At any other time she might have thrown in a sarcastic *We've missed you*, but Ty Allardyce was being deadly serious, so she settled for, 'I expect you keep in touch by phone.'

He nodded. 'Which in no way prepared me for the shock I received when I made what was meant to be a snatched visit here a couple of weeks ago.'

'Ah—you're talking…Ash?'

'You've noticed the change in him?'

Who could fail to? 'He's—not ill?'

'Not in the accepted sense.'

'Did Leanne do this to him?' She voiced her thoughts, and saw his mouth tighten.

'I couldn't believe that some money-grabbing female could so wreck a man, but—' He broke off, then resumed, 'Anyhow, I felt there was no way I could return to London. Not then. Not now—without your help.'

'I'll do anything I can, naturally.'

'Good,' he said. 'The job is yours.'

She stared at this man who she had to admit she was starting to like—though she was fully prepared to believe that shock did funny things to people, but still felt no further forward. 'Er—and the job is what, exactly?'

'I thought I'd just said,' Ty replied, 'I want you to be Ash's companion.'

Her mouth fell open. 'You want me to be your brother's *companion*?' she echoed.

'I'll pay you, of course,' Ty answered, seeing absolutely nothing untoward in what he was proposing.

'You want me to be his paid companion?' she questioned again, as it started to sink in. 'His—his minder?'

'No, not minder!' Ty answered shortly. 'I've explained how things are.'

'Not really you haven't,' Phinn stated, and was on the receiving end of an impatient look.

'The situation is,' he explained heavily, 'that while I can do certain parts of my job in my study, via computer and telephone, other matters require my presence in London or some other capital. I've been down here for two weeks more than I originally intended already. And, while I have a pressing need to get back to town, I still don't feel ready to leave Ash on his own.'

Phinn thought about it. 'You think I might be the person to take over from you for a while?'

'Can you think of anyone better than someone who has actually risked their own life for him, as you did today?'

'I don't know about that,' she mumbled.

JESSICA STEELE 55

'Ash likes you. He enjoyed talking to you the other day.'

'Um—that was the day you told me to leave him alone, to—'

'I was angry,' Ty admitted. 'I didn't want another Hawkins finishing off what your cousin had done to him. But that was before I was able to reason that he was still so ensnared by her that other women just don't exist for him. Frankly, Ash wouldn't fancy you even if you *did* use your beauty to try to hook him.'

Beauty? Hook him? Charming! At that point Phinn was in two minds about whether or not she wanted the job. She felt sorry for Ash—of course she did. As for her cousin…she was feeling quite angry with Leanne. But…then Phinn thought of Ruby, and at the thought of a stable *and* a paddock there was no question but that she wanted the job.

'I haven't the first idea what a paid companion is supposed to do… I mean, what would I have to do? You wouldn't expect me to take him down to the pub and get drunk with him every night, I hope?'

'You like beer?' he asked sharply.

'No!' she shot straight back.

'You'd been drinking this afternoon,' he retorted, obviously not caring to be lied to. 'There was a smell of beer on your breath.'

'Honestly!' she exclaimed. And she was thinking of *working* for this man who could sniff out beer at a hundred paces! But what choice did she have? 'If you must know, I hate the stuff. But I've been having a courtesy swig out of Idris Owens' beer tankard ever since I was ten years old—it's a sort of tradition, each time I go to the farrier. It would have been churlish to refuse his offer when I took Ruby to have her hooves checked over by him this afternoon.'

For a moment Ty Allardyce said nothing, just sat there looking at her. Then he said quietly, 'Rather than hurt his feelings, you quaffed ale that you've no particular liking for?'

'So what does that make me?' she challenged, expecting something pretty pithy in reply.

But, to her surprise, he replied in that same quiet tone. 'I think it makes you a rather nice kind of person.' And she was struck again by the change in him from the man she had thought he was.

'Yes, well…' she said abruptly—grief, she'd be going soft in the head about him in a minute. Buck up, she instructed herself. This man could be iron-hard and unyielding without any trouble. Hadn't she witnessed that for herself? 'So I'm—er—to take over the sort of guardianship of Ash from you while you—um—go about your business?'

'Not quite,' Ty replied. 'What I believe Ash needs just now is to be with someone who will be a sensitive ear for him when he needs to talk. Someone to take him out of himself when he looks like becoming a little melancholy.'

'You think I've got a sensitive ear?'

Again he looked steadily at her. 'You'll do,' he said. And he would have left it at that, but there were questions queuing up in Phinn's mind.

'You think it will take as long as six months for Ash to—um—get back to being his old self?'

'Hopefully nowhere near as long. Who knows? Whatever—I'm prepared to guarantee stabling and a place for you to rest your head for the whole six months.'

'Fine,' she said.

'You'll start tomorrow?'

And how! 'You'd better let me have your phone number,' she requested, overjoyed, now it had had time to sink in, that by the look of it Ruby was going to have a proper stable and a paddock all to herself.

'Why would you want my phone number?' Ty asked shortly.

'Oh, for goodness' sake!' she erupted at her new boss. 'So I can ring Ash and ask him to come and pick me up with my belongings. I can bring Ruby over later.'

'You want to inspect her accommodation first?'

'I'd—er—have put it a little more tactfully,' she mumbled. 'But, yes, that's the general idea. I could still ask Mickie if you don't want Ash to do it.'

'Who's Mickie?'

'He lives in the village. He's a bit eccentric, but he has a heart of gold. He—er—' She broke off—that was more than he needed to know.

She quickly realised that she should have known better. '"He—er—" what?'

Phinn gave a resigned sigh. 'Well, if you must know, I'd already arranged for Mickie to take my cases and bits and pieces up to Honeysuckle Farm for me tomorrow.'

Ty Allardyce shook his head, as though she was a new kind of species to him. 'Presumably he would have kept quiet about your whereabouts?'

'Well, there you are,' she said briskly, about nothing, and then fell headlong when, in the same bracing tone, she said, 'Had I not sold my car, I…' Her voice trailed away. 'Well, I did,' she added quickly. And then, hurriedly attempting to close the interview—or whatever it was, 'So I'll get Mickie to—'

'You sold your car?' Ty Allardyce took up.

'Yep.' He didn't need to hear more.

And nor did he, she discovered. Because what this clever man did not know he was astute enough to decipher and guess at. 'According to my lawyers, you paid a whole whack of back rent before you handed in the keys to the farm,' he commented slowly. Adding, 'Had I thought about it at all, I'd have assumed that the money came from your father's estate. But—' he looked at her sharply '—it didn't, did it?'

She shrugged. 'What did I need a car for? I thought I'd got a steady job here—no need to look for work further afield. Besides, I couldn't leave Ruby on her own all day.' Phinn halted, she'd had enough of talking about herself. 'Have you told Ash that you were going to offer me a job?'

Ty looked at her unspeaking for some moments, and then replied, 'No.'

She saw it might be a little awkward if Ash objected strongly. 'How do you think he'll take my moving in to be his companion?' No point in ducking the question. If Ash did not want her there, then the next six months could be pretty miserable all round.

'My brother feels things very deeply,' Ty began. 'He has been hurt—badly hurt. In my view it would be easier for him if he didn't know the true reason for your being at the Hall.'

'I wouldn't be able to lie to him,' Phinn said quickly. 'I'm not very good at telling lies.'

'You wouldn't have to lie.'

Phinn looked into steady grey eyes and felt somewhat perplexed. 'What, then?' she asked. 'I can't just ring him out of the blue and ask him to come and get me.'

'It won't be a problem,' Ty assured her. 'Ash knows that you and Ruby have to leave here. I'll tell him that, apropos of you having nowhere to go, I called to thank you for what you did today and offered you a temporary home.'

Phinn's eyes widened. 'You think he'll believe such philanthropy?' she queried—and discovered that her hint of sarcasm was not lost on him.

'My stars, I pity the poor man who ends up with *you*!' he muttered under his breath, but then agreed, 'Normally I doubt he'd believe it for a moment. But, apart from him not being too concerned about anything very much just now, he's as grateful to you as I am that you were where you were today.' The matter settled as far as he was concerned, he took out his wallet, extracted his business card, wrote several numbers on it and, standing up, handed it to her.

Phinn glanced at the card in her hand and read that he had

given her his office number, his mobile number, the phone number of his London home and the one she had asked for—the number of the Hall.

'No need to have gone raving mad,' she commented. She had only wanted one telephone number, for goodness' sake!

'Just in case,' he said, and she realised he meant her to ring him if she felt things were going badly for Ash. 'Feel free to ring me at any time,' he added.

'Right,' she agreed, and stood up too. She found he was too close and, feeling a mite odd for no reason, took a step away.

'How are you feeling now?' he thought to ask before he turned to the door.

'Feeling?' For a moment she wasn't with him.

Without more ado he caught hold of both of her hands. When, his touch making her tingle, she would have snatched her hands back, he held on to them. 'You're not shaking,' he observed—and then she *was* with him.

'Oh, I think the shock has passed now,' she informed him, only then starting to wonder if this man—this complex kind of man—had stayed talking with her as long as he had so as to be on hand if she looked like going into full-blown shock. 'You're kinder than I thought,' she blurted out, quite without thinking—and abruptly had her hands dropped like hot coals.

'Spread that around and I'll have to kill you,' he said shortly. And that was it. He was gone.

Starting to only half-believe that Ty Allardyce had been in the flat and made that staggering, not to say wonderful job and accommodation offer for her and Ruby, Phinn went quickly to the window that overlooked the stableyard.

He was there. She had not dreamt it. Ty Allardyce was in the stableyard talking to Geraldine Walton. What was more, Geraldine was smiling her head off. Never had Phinn seen her look more animated or more pleasant.

Phinn added 'charm' to Ty Allardyce's list of accomplishments, and wondered what he was talking to Geraldine about. Keeping out of sight, she watched for a minute or so more, and then the two of them disappeared.

While they were gone she observed that there was a pick-up vehicle in the yard that did not belong to the stables. She assumed that Ty Allardyce had driven over in it.

She soon saw that her assumption was correct. When he and Geraldine Walton appeared again, he was hauling a bale of straw and Geraldine was wheeling a bale of hay. Phinn watched as the two bales were loaded onto the pick-up. She kept out of sight as the two disappeared again, and then reappeared with the special feed Phinn herself had bought for Ruby, who needed it on account of her teeth not being what they once had been.

Feeling little short of amazed, Phinn watched as the two chatted a little while longer, before Ty got into the pick-up and drove away.

Was he a mover or was he a mover? My heavens, it had all been cut and dried as far as he was concerned before he had even left Broadlands! Ty Allardyce needed someone trustworthy to keep his brother company while he returned to the business he had already neglected for far too long, and he had it all planned out before he had come to see her!

While he might not have cared for her standing up to him over her right to trespass, it was plain that in his view, when it came to being trustworthy with his brother, there was no higher recommendation than that she had that day taken a header into the pool to get his brother out when Ash had got into difficulties. Plan made, all that he'd needed to do was come and see her and—as it were—make her an offer she couldn't refuse.

That he had known in advance that she would not refuse his offer was evidenced by the fact he had driven over in the pick-up. Efficient or what? Since he would be at the stables, he might as well collect a few things and save an extra journey later.

Feeling a little bit stunned by the man's efficiency, Phinn went out to check on Ruby. Inevitably, it seemed, she bumped into Geraldine Walton.

'You didn't say you were starting work up at the Hall?' Geraldine commented, and seemed more relaxed than she had before.

Phinn felt a little stumped as to how to reply. There was no way she was going to reveal to anyone the true nature of her job at the Hall. On the other hand, given that Geraldine could be tough when she had to be, she did not want to part with bad feelings.

'I'm just hoping my secretarial skills aren't too rusty,' she answered lightly. It was the best she could do at a moment's notice, and she hoped it would suffice as a white lie. 'Must go and check on Ruby,' she added with a smile, and went quickly on.

Ruby came over to her as soon as she saw her, and Phinn told her all about the move tomorrow, and about the nice new paddock all to herself. Ruby nuzzled into her neck appreciatively—and Phinn came near to feeling relaxed for the first time in an age.

She stayed talking to Ruby for quite some while, and was in fact still with her when she thought that perhaps she had given Ty plenty of time in which to tell his brother that from tomorrow on they were to have a house guest.

Realising she had left her mobile phone and the phone numbers Ty had given her back in the flat, she parted from Ruby briefly while she nipped back to the accommodation she would be vacating in the morning.

Finding the card, she dialled the number of the Hall and, for no known reason expecting that Ash would be the one to answer her call, was a little nonplussed to hear Ty's voice. 'Allardyce,' he said, and she knew straight away that it was him.

'Oh, hello, Ty—er—Mr Allardyce,' she stumbled, feeling a fool.

'Ty,' he invited, and asked, 'Did you want to speak with Ash?'

'If I may,' she replied primly. And that was it. A few minutes later Ash was on the line.

'I wanted to ring you,' he said, before she could say a word. 'We hadn't got your number, but I wanted to thank you so much, Phinn, for what you did today. I didn't get a chance before. When I think—'

'That's all right, Ash,' she butted in. 'Er—actually, Ty stopped by to thank me. Um—I think you must have told him about my need to move from here?'

'I'm glad I did. Ty says he knows we can never repay you, but that he's offered you and your horse temporary accommodation here until you can sort something out.'

'You don't mind?'

'Good Lord, no! Ty's suggested I get busy sorting out the old stable in the morning.'

'I'll come and help!' Phinn volunteered promptly. 'Actually, I'm without wheels, so if you could come and collect me and some of my stuff, it…?'

'I owe you—big-time. Nine o'clock suit?'

Phinn went to bed that night with her head buzzing. She barely knew where to start when she thought of all that had happened that day. Drinking beer in the forge! That ghastly picture of Ash in trouble! His complex brother! His amazing offer! All in all, today had been one almighty day for huge surprises.

Strangely, though, as she lay in the dark going over everything in her head, it was Ty Allardyce who figured most largely in her thoughts. He could be hard, he could be bossy—overbearing, even—but he could be kind too. Complex did she say? Ty Allardyce was something else again.

She remembered the way he had taken her hands in his, and

recalled the way she had tingled all over. Don't be ridiculous, she instructed herself. Just look forward to going to Broadlands Hall to be a companion to Ash so that Ty can get back to the work he so obviously loves.

From her point of view, things couldn't be better. When she thought about it, a return to Honeysuckle Farm had been a far from ideal solution. Both she and Ruby would fare much better at Broadlands. They were truly most fortunate.

But—Phinn fidgeted in her bed—why was she feeling just a little disturbed? As if there was something not quite right somewhere?

CHAPTER FOUR

PHINN was up and about long before Ash called for her the next day. She had tended to Ruby's requirements earlier, and spent her time waiting for Ash in folding Ruby's blankets and in getting the mare's belongings together.

Turning Ruby out into the field for the last time, Phinn cleaned out her stall so that Geraldine would have nothing to complain over. But even though she felt sure Ruby's new accommodation would be adequate, she still wanted to look it over before she moved her.

A little after nine Ash drove into the yard and found her waiting for him. He looked dreadfully tired, Phinn thought, as though his nights were long and tortuous.

'Ready?' he asked, pushing out a smile.

'There's rather a lot to cart over,' she mentioned apologetically.

They had almost finished loading the pick-up when Geraldine Walton appeared, and Phinn introduced the two. 'You manage the estate, I believe?' Geraldine commented pleasantly, clearly having been in the area long enough to have picked up village gossip.

'Something like that,' Ash muttered, and hefted the last of Phinn's cases into the back of the pick-up. 'That it?' he asked Phinn.

She smiled at him and, feeling that he had perhaps been a little off with Geraldine, smiled at her too. 'I'll be over for Ruby later,' she confirmed.

'She'll be fine until then. No need to rush back. I'll keep an eye on her,' Geraldine promised.

A minute or so later and Ash was driving the pick-up out of the stableyard. Her job, Phinn realised, had begun. 'Er—Ty gone back to London?' she enquired—more to get Ash to start talking than because she had any particular interest in his brother.

But Ash took his glance from the road briefly to give her what she could only describe as a knowing look as he enquired, 'Didn't he phone you before he left?'

There was no reason why he should phone, as far as Phinn was aware, and she almost said as much—but that was before, on thinking about that knowing look, the most astonishing thought hit her! It couldn't be—could it?

She tried to look at the situation from Ash's angle. Given that she was unable to tell Ash that the real reason she was coming to live at the Hall was in order to keep an eye on him and, unbeknown to him, be his companion, did Ash think that there was more in his brother's invitation for her to stay at the Hall than his gratitude after yesterday's events?

She opened her mouth to tell Ash bluntly that there was nothing going on between her and his brother Ty, nor likely to be, but the moment had passed. Then she was glad she had said nothing; she had obviously got it wrong. In actual fact, when she thought of the glamorous females that Ty probably dated, she was doubly glad she had said nothing. Far better to keep her mouth shut than to make a fool of herself.

Ash drove straight to the stable. There were bits and pieces of packing cases outside, she noticed as they drove up. 'I was supposed to have the stable empty before you got here, but I—er—got kind of sidetracked,' Ash excused.

'Well, with two of us I don't suppose it will take us very

long,' Phinn said brightly, more concerned with having a look inside than anything else just then.

Taking into account that there were more packing cases inside, plus an old scrubbed kitchen table and other items which she guessed had come out of the Hall when it had been modernised, the stable was more than adequate—even to the water tap on one wall. Indeed, once she had got it all spruced up, brushed out, and with fresh straw put down, it would be little short of luxury for Ruby.

'Roll your sleeves up time!' she announced.

'You don't want to go into the house and check on your room first?'

Where she laid her head that night was immaterial to Phinn just then. Her first priority was to get Ruby settled. 'I'm sure it will be fine,' she answered. 'Will you help?'

Reluctantly at first, Ash started bundling boxes out of the way. And then gradually he began to take over. 'Leave that one,' he ordered at one stage, when she tried to manhandle what had been some part of a kitchen cabinet. 'I'll move that.' And later, 'What we're going to have to do is to take this lot down to the tip.'

Sacrilege! Phinn took out her phone and pressed out Mickie Yates's number. With luck she'd get him before he went for lunch, and she needed to talk to him anyway.

She was in luck. He was home. 'Mickie? Phinn Hawkins.'

'I haven't forgotten,' he replied, a smile in his voice. 'Three o'clock.'

'Change of plan,' she stated. 'I'm—er—working and staying at the Hall for a while.' She could feel Ash's eyes on her, and felt awkward. 'The thing is, we're clearing out the stable for Ruby. Can you find homes for some kitchen units and the like that still have some life in them, do you think?'

'Today?'

'That would be good.'

'An hour?'

'That would be brilliant.'

'See you, lovely girl.'

Putting her phone away after making the call, Phinn looked up to find that Ash was staring at her. 'You're working here?' he enquired.

She went red. Grief—what *was* it about these Allardyce brothers? 'Shut up—and help me move this,' she ordered— and to her great delight, after a stunned moment she saw a half-grin break on Ash's features. It seemed an age since she had last seen him smile.

She was delighted, but a moment or two later she distinctly heard him comment, 'She blushes, and Ty says he'll try and get back tonight...' And then she heard him deliberately sing a snatch of 'Love Is in the Air'.

'Ash,' she warned.

'What?' he asked.

What could she say? 'Nothing,' she replied.

'Sorry,' he apologized. 'Am I treading all over your tender feelings?'

There was no answer to that either. 'Now, where did I put that yard broom?' she said instead, but knew then she had to believe that Ash thought that there might be something going on between her and his elder brother.

What? After only seeing her once? Though on second thought, how did she know that since Ty did not want Ash to know the real reason she was there, Ty had *not* instigated or at least allowed Ash to nurture such thoughts? He could quite truthfully have told Ash that, apart from the time she had called at the house with his camera, they had bumped into each other on a couple of other occasions and stopped for a chat.

That, 'Get off my land!' and a threat to summons her for trespass hardly constituted 'a chat' was neither here nor there.

But it was plain Ash thought that there was more to Ty inviting her to live under his roof and offering to stable her horse than appeared on the surface. Hadn't she herself asked Ty, 'You think he'll believe such philanthropy?' Clearly Ash did not. What Ash had chosen to believe was that she was some kind of would-be girlfriend to his brother. And, bearing in mind that she could not tell Ash the truth, there was nothing she could do to disabuse him of the idea.

Having reached the conclusion that Ash was not so down as she had at first thought, she saw the more cheerful mood he had been in while they had been busy start to fall away once the stable was empty of impedimenta and Mickie Yates had called and carted everything away.

'I think I'll take a shortcut through the spinney and collect Ruby,' Phinn said lightly. Straw was down; water was in the trough they had unearthed and scrubbed.

'I'll drive you there if you like?' he offered, but she knew that his heart was not in it.

For a moment she wondered if the fact that Geraldine had the look of her cousin and it would upset him had anything to do with it. If so, perhaps it would be kinder not to trigger memories of Leanne should Geraldine be about.

'No need,' she answered gently. But, bearing in mind that he had seemed happier when working, she went on. 'Though if you're strolling down anywhere near the paddock you might check if it's Ruby-friendly for me.'

Ash nodded and went on his way. By then Phinn was learning to trust Ty enough that if he thought the paddock was suitable for Ruby, there would be no stray barbed wire or plant-life dangerous to horses.

She was feeling sorely in need of a shower and a change of clothes, but Ruby still had to be Phinn's first priority. She wanted her away from the other horses, and so went as quickly as she could to get her.

First she was met by Geraldine—a smiling Geraldine—who offered to supply her with hay and straw from her own supplies. 'You can have it for the price I pay for it,' she offered pleasantly.

Thanking her, feeling cheered, Phinn went looking for Ruby, and was instantly rewarded when Ruby spotted her straight away and came over to her as fast as she could. 'Come on, darling,' Phinn murmured to her softly. 'Have I got a lovely surprise for you.'

Ruby did not have much of an appetite, and after staying with her for a while as she got used to her new surroundings, Phinn left her and went over to the house.

She went in though the kitchen door and at once saw Mrs Starkey, who was at the sink scrubbing new potatoes. She smiled when she saw her. 'Come in, Phinn, come in. Your room's all ready for you.'

'I hope I haven't put you to a lot of trouble?' Phinn apologised.

'None at all! It will be nice having you in the house,' Mrs Starkey answered cheerfully, more than happy, it seemed, in her now streamlined kitchen. 'Dinner's usually about seven-thirty, but I've made you a sandwich to tide you over. Or you could have some soup, or a salad, or…'

'A sandwich will do fine, Mrs Starkey. What I need most is a shower and a change of clothes.'

Mrs Starkey washed and dried her hands. 'Come on, then. I'll show you your room. Ashley came in earlier with your belongings and took them up for you. I hope it's all right? I've had your cardboard boxes put in the storeroom, but…'

'That's lovely.' Phinn thanked her, and as they climbed the winding staircase asked, 'Where is Ash? Do you know?'

For a brief second or two the housekeeper lost her smile. 'I think he's taken himself off for a walk. He didn't want anything to eat, and he barely touched his breakfast.' She shook her head. 'I don't know,' she said, more to herself than anything as they went along the landing.

Phinn was unsure what, if anything, to answer. But she was saved having to make a reply when Mrs Starkey halted at one of the bedroom doors.

'Here we are,' she said, opening the door and standing back for Phinn to go in. 'I hope it's to your liking.'

Liking! 'Oh, Mrs Starkey, it's lovely!' she cried. And it was.

'I'll leave you to get settled in and have your shower.' Mrs Starkey seemed as pleased as Phinn herself.

Phinn stood in the centre of the recently refurbished room and turned very slowly around. The huge, high-ceilinged, light and airy room, with its own modernised bathroom, was more of a bedsitting room than anything. One wall had been given over to built-in wardrobes, with a dressing table in between—far more wardrobe space than she would ever need, Phinn mused. And there was a padded stool in delicate cream and antique gold in front of the dressing table area that had a light above it.

The bed was a double bed, with a cream and antique gold bedcover. At the foot of the bed was a padded cream ottoman, and further in front of that a padded antique gold-coloured chaise longue. A small round table reposed to the side of it, and to the side of that stood a small matching padded chair.

Remembering her cold and draughty bedroom at Honeysuckle Farm, where she would have been returning today but for the turn of events, Phinn could only stare in wonder. She took another slow turn around again—and she had thought Ruby's accommodation luxurious!

Feeling a little stunned, and thinking that she would not want to leave when her six months at Broadlands Hall were over, Phinn went to inspect the bathroom. She was not disappointed. There must be a snag, she pondered. And, stripping off, stepped into the shower—certain that the plumbing or some such would prove faulty.

It proved not faulty. The water was fine, as hot or not as she would have wished.

Refreshed from her shower, Phinn quickly dressed in some clean clothes and, with her thoughts on introducing Ruby to the paddock, swiftly left her room—she could unpack later. She went to the kitchen.

'Tea or coffee?' Mrs Starkey asked as soon as she saw her. And only then did Phinn realise that she felt quite parched.

'Actually, I'd better go and see to Ruby. But I'll have a glass of water,' she answered. No time to wait for tea or coffee.

'Juice?' Mrs Starkey offered, and as Phinn glanced at the motherly woman she suddenly felt as if she had come home.

'Juice would be lovely,' she replied gratefully. And while she drank her juice she saw Mrs Starkey fold her sandwich up in a paper napkin.

'Our John never used to have a moment to breathe either,' she remarked, handing over the sandwich with a smile.

'Thank you, Mrs Starkey,' Phinn said, and had her empty glass taken out of her hand when she would have taken it over to the sink and washed it, and the sandwich pressed in its place.

Life was suddenly good. Phinn all at once realised that she was feeling the best she had felt since her father had died. Now, who did she thank for that? Ty, Ash, Mrs Starkey—or just the passage of time?

Whatever—just enjoy.

Another plus was that Ruby appeared a little hungry. Some of her special feed had gone anyway. Phinn took her down to the fenced-off paddock, checked she had water, and sat on the fence eating her sandwich while Ruby found her way around.

After a while Phinn got down from the fence. Ruby was not her only concern, but this was her first day, and apart from having to clear out the stables and make everything ready, Phinn had not got into any sort of pattern as yet. But she was mindful that she should be looking out for Ash.

Leaving Ruby, Phinn went looking for him. He had gone for a walk, Mrs Starkey had said. But that had been hours ago.

Phinn had gone some way, and was near to the pool when through the trees she caught a glimpse of something blue. If memory served, Ash had been wearing a blue shirt that morning. Should she leave him or keep him company?

The matter was solved when she recalled that she was being *employed* to keep Ash company. She went forward, making sufficient noise so as not to suddenly startle him. She found him sitting on the bank, his expression bleak, and her heart went out to him. How long had he been sitting there, staring at the water without really seeing anything but her cousin?

'Can you believe this glorious weather?' she asked, for something to say.

'Get Ruby over okay?' Ash roused himself to ask.

'The paddock's a dream!'

'Good,' he replied politely, and made no objection when she decided to sit down beside him.

Sitting down beside him was one thing. Now she had to think of something to talk about! 'Are you really the estate manager?' she asked, playing the companion role by ear.

'It doesn't need much managing,' he replied.

'You reckon?'

'You know differently?' he countered, and she sensed an interest—slight, but a spark of interest nevertheless.

'No. Not really,' she answered hurriedly. 'Only…'

'Only?'

'Well, I couldn't help noticing the other day when I was walking through Pixie End Wood that there are one or two trees that need taking out and new ones planting in their place.'

'Where's Pixie End Wood?'

Phinn worked on that spark of interest. 'If I'm not too busy with Ruby tomorrow I'll take you there, if you like?'

He nodded, but she knew his interest was waning. 'How's Leanne?' he asked, totally unexpectedly.

Oh, Ash. Phinn knew, just as she knew that there was nothing she could do to help, that Ash was bleeding a little inside. 'We're not in contact,' she replied. 'It's like that with relatives sometimes. You rarely ever see each other except for weddings and—' She broke off, spears of sad memory still able to dart in unexpectedly and stop her in her tracks.

'I'm sorry.' Ash, like the normally thoughtful person he was, sensed what she had not been able to say. The last time Leanne had surfaced had been to attend Phinn's father's funeral. 'Come on,' he said, shaking off his apathy in the face of Phinn having a weak moment. 'Let's go and see how Ruby likes her new digs.'

By early evening Phinn was in her room again, wondering at her stroke of luck at being at Broadlands. Because her watch had stopped working she was having to guess at the time, but she thought it had been around six that evening when she and Ash had returned to the house. She had come straight to her room and begun finding homes for her belongings.

She had been surprised, however, when opening a drawer in her bedside table, to find an envelope with her name on it. When she had opened it, it had been to extract a cheque written and signed in Ty's firm hand, for what she presumed was her first month's wages.

She felt a little hot about the ears when, never having been paid in advance before, she wondered if Ty had guessed at the parlous state of her finances. The fact that the cheque was for more than she would have thought too made her realise the importance he gave to his brother's welfare. In his view Ash needed a companion when Ty could not be there himself— and he was prepared to pay up-front for that cover.

Knowing that she was going to do her best to fulfil that role, Phinn, surmising that 'companions' probably ate with the

family, went to assess her wardrobe. She had several decent
dresses, but she had no wish to be 'over the top'. Jeans were
out, she guessed, so she settled for a smart pair of white
trousers and topped them with a loose-fitting short blue kaftan.

It seemed an age since she had last used anything but mois-
turiser on her face, but she thought a dab of powder and a
smear of lipstick might not be a bad idea. Why, as she was
studying her finished appearance, she should think of Ty
Allardyce she had no idea.

She hadn't seen him since yesterday. Nor had she heard
him come home. Would he be there at dinner? Did she want
him there at dinner? Oh, for goodness' sake—what the blazes
did it matter where he was? He—

Someone tapping on her door caused her to break off her
thoughts.

And, on her answering the door, who should be standing
there but none other than the subject of her thoughts? She felt
suddenly shy.

'Hungry?' Ty enquired easily.

She at once discounted that she was in any way shy of him.
'Mrs Starkey said dinner was around seven-thirty,' Phinn responded. Shy or not, she glanced away from those steady
grey eyes and raised her left hand to check the time on her
wrist. No watch!

'It's seven forty-five,' Ty informed her.

'It isn't!' she exclaimed. Where had the day gone?

'You look ready to me,' he observed. And, stepping back,
he clearly expected her to join him.

A smile lit the inside of her. Ty must have come up the
stairs purposely to collect her. 'Busy day?' she enquired, leaving her room and going along the landing with him.

'Not as physically busy as you, from what I hear. Ash tells
me you put him to shame.'

She shook her head. 'Once Ash got into his stride it was

he who did the lion's share of lumping and bumping,' she stated, and saw that Ty looked pleased.

'And your friend Mickie Yates came and took everything away?'

'You don't mind?'

'Good Lord, why would I?' Ty replied, and startled her completely when, totally away from what they had been talking about, he shot a question at her. 'Where's your watch?'

Taken by surprise, she answered, 'It got wet,' quite without thinking. And was halfway down the stairs when Ty stepped in front of her, turned and halted—causing her to have to halt too.

'You mean you forgot to take it off when you did your Olympian dive yesterday?'

'I can't think of everything!' she exclaimed. 'It will be all right when it dries out,' she added off-handedly, knowing that it would never work again, but not wanting to make an issue of it. It hadn't been an expensive watch, after all.

'As you remarked—you're no good at telling lies.' He neatly tripped her up.

What could she do? Say? She gave him a cheeky grin. 'The paddock is lovely,' she informed him.

He shook his head slightly, the way she noticed he did when he was a little unsure of what to make of her.

Dinner was a pleasant meal, though Phinn observed that Ash ate very little. For all that the ham salad with buttered potatoes and a rather fine onion tart was very palatable, he seemed to be eating it for form's sake rather than because he was enjoying it.

'Did you find time to get into the estate office today?' Ty, having included her in all the conversation so far, put a question to his brother.

'Who wants to be indoors on a day like today?' Ash replied. 'I'll see what I can do tomorrow,' he added. Ty did not press him, or look in any way put out. And then Ash was confessing, 'Actually, I think Phinn would make a better estate manager than me.'

Phinn opened her mouth, ready with a disclaimer, and then noticed Ty's glance had switched to her. He was plainly interested in his brother's comment.

'I'm beginning to think that nothing Phinn does will surprise me,' he said. 'But—' he glanced back to Ash '—why, particularly?'

'Apparently I'm being taken on a tour of Pixie End Wood tomorrow. Phinn tells me there are a couple of trees there that need felling, and new ones planting.'

Ty's glance was back on her, and she was sure she looked guilty. She knew that he was now aware that her trespassing had not been limited to the few places where he had witnessed it.

When, after dinner, a move was made to the drawing room, Phinn would by far have preferred to have gone to the stable. But, even though she felt that Ty would not expect her to be on 'companion duty' when he was home to keep his brother company, she was aware that there were certain courtesies to be observed when living in someone else's home.

And so, thinking that to spend another ten minutes with the Allardyce brothers wouldn't hurt, she went along to the drawing room with them. But she was hardly through the door when she stopped dead in her tracks.

'Grandmother Hawkins' table!' she exclaimed, all the other plush furnishings and antique furniture fading from her sight as she recognised the much-loved, much-polished, small round table that had been theirs up until 'needs must', as her father had called their impecunious moments, and the table had been sold.

'Grandmother Hawkins?' Ash enquired. 'You mean you once owned that table?'

Grandmother Hawkins had handed it down to Phinn's parents early in their marriage, when they'd had little furniture of their own. They had later inherited the rest of her antiques. 'It's—er—lovely, isn't it?' she replied, feeling awkward and wishing that she hadn't said anything.

'You're sure it's yours? Ty bought it in London.'

'I'm sure. We sold it—it wasn't stolen. We—er...' She had been about to say how it had been about the last one of their antiques to go, but there was no need for anyone to know of their hard-up moments. 'It was probably sold to a dealer who sold it on.'

'And you recognise it?'

'I should do—it was my Saturday morning job to polish it. I've been polishing it since I was about three years old.' A gentle smile of happy remembering lifted her mouth. 'My father's initials are lightly carved underneath. We both got into trouble when he showed me how to carve mine in too. My mother could never erase them—no matter how much she tried.'

'The table obviously holds very happy memories for you,' Ty put in quietly.

'I had the happiest of childhoods,' she replied, and suddenly felt embarrassed at talking of things they could not possibly be interested in.

'You were upset when your father sold it?' Ty enquired, his eyes watching her.

She looked at him in surprise, the blue top she wore reflecting the deepening blue of her eyes. How had he known it was her father who had sold the table and not her mother? 'He was my father!' she protested.

'And as such could do no wrong?' Ty suggested quietly.

She looked away from him. It was true. In her eyes her father had never been able to do anything wrong. 'Would you mind very much if I went and took a look at Ruby?'

She flicked a quick glance back to Ty, but his expression was inscrutable. She took that to mean that he would not mind, and was on her way.

Ruby had had the best of days, and seemed truly happy and

content in her new abode. Phinn stayed with her, talking softly to her as she did every evening. And as she chatted to her Phinn started once more to come near to being content herself.

She was still with Ruby when the mare's ears pricked up and Phinn knew that they were about to have company.

'How's she settled in?' Ty asked, coming into the large stable and joining them.

'I think we can safely say that she loves her new home.'

Ty nodded. Then asked, 'How about you?'

'Who could fail to love it here? My room's a dream!'

He looked pleased. 'Any problems I should know about?' he asked. 'Don't be afraid to say—no matter how small,' he added.

'It's only my first day. Nothing untoward, but—' She broke off, caught out by the memory of Ash giving her that knowing look that morning.

'What?' Ty asked.

My heavens, was he sharp! 'Nothing,' she answered. But then she thought that perhaps she *should* mention it. 'Well, the thing is, I think Ash seems to have got hold of the idea that—um—you and I—are—er—starting some sort of...' Grief, she knew she was going red again.

'Some sort of...?' Ty questioned, not sparing her blushes.

And that annoyed her. 'Well, if you must know, I think he thinks we're starting some sort of romantic attachment.' There—it was out. She waited for him to look totally astounded at the idea. But to her astonishment he actually started to grin. She stared at him, her heart going all fluttery for no good reason.

Then Ty was sobering, and to her amazement he was confessing, 'My fault entirely, I'm afraid.'

'Your fault?'

'Forgive me, Phinn?' he requested, not for a moment looking sorry about anything. 'I could tell the way his mind was working when I told him I'd asked you to stay with us for a while.'

Phinn stared at him. 'But you didn't tell him—?' she gasped.

'I thought it better not to disabuse him of the notion,' Ty cut in.

'Why on earth not?' she bridled.

'Now, don't get cross,' Ty admonished. 'You know quite well the real reason why you're here.'

'To be Ash's companion.'

'Right,' Ty agreed. 'You're here to keep him company—but he's not to know about it. From where I'm viewing it, Ash has got enough to handle without having the added weight of feeling under too much of an obligation for what you did for him yesterday. He's indebted to you—of course he is. We both are,' Ty went on. 'The alternative—what could have happened had you not been around and had the guts to do what you did—just doesn't bear thinking about. But he's under enough emotional pressure. I just thought it might take some of the pressure from him if he could more cheerfully think that, while things might be going wrong for him in his personal life, I—his big brother— was having a better time of it and had invited you here more because I was smitten than because of what we both owe you.'

Despite herself, Phinn could see the logic of what Ty had just said. She remembered how down Ash had seemed when she had come across him on the bank today. She recalled that bleak expression on his face and had to agree. Ty's brother did not need any extra burden just now.

'As long as you don't expect me to give you a cuddle every now and then,' she retorted sniffily at last.

She saw his lips twitch and turned away, and, feeling funny inside, showed an interest in Ruby.

'As pleasant as one of your cuddles would surely be, I'll try to hold down my expectations,' Ty replied smoothly, and for a minute she did not like him again, because again he was making her feel a fool. All too plainly the sky would fall in before he would want to be anywhere near cuddling distance with *her*.

'Are you home tomorrow?' she turned to enquire, thinking that as it was Saturday he might well be.

'Want to take me to Pixie End Wood too?'

She gave him a hostile look, bit down on a reply of *Yes, and leave you there*, and settled for, 'You intimated you'd neglected your work in London. I merely wondered if you'd be going back to catch up.'

'You don't like me, do you?'

At this moment, no. She shrugged her shoulders. 'I can take you or leave you,' she replied, to let him know that she was not bothered about him one way or the other. But flicking a glance to him, she saw she had amused him. Not in the least offended, he looked more likely to laugh than to be heartbroken.

'How's the…Ruby?' He made one of his lightning switches of conversation.

Ah, that was different. Taking the talk away from herself and on to Ruby was far preferable. 'She's happy—really settled in well. She's eaten more today than she has in a while. And this stable, the paddock—they're a dream for her.'

'Good,' Ty commented, and then, dipping his hand into his trouser pocket, he pulled out a wristwatch and handed it to her. 'You'll need one of these until your own dries out,' he remarked.

Having taken it from him, Phinn stared at the handsome gentleman's watch in her hand. 'I can't…' she began, trying to give it back to him.

'It's a spare.' He refused to take it. 'And only a loan.'

She looked at him, feeling stumped. The phrase 'hoist with her own petard' came to mind. She had told him her watch would be all right again once it had dried out—but he knew that, no matter how dry it was, it would never be serviceable again.

'I'll let you have it back in due time.' She accepted it with what dignity she could muster, and was glad when, with a kind pat to Ruby's flank, Ty Allardyce bade her, *'Adieu,'* and went.

Phinn stayed with Ruby, wondering what it was about the man that disturbed her so. In truth, she had never met any man who could make her so annoyed with him one second and yet on the point of laughter the next.

Eventually she said goodnight to Ruby and returned to the house, musing that it had been thoughtful of Ty to loan her a watch. How many times that day had she automatically checked her left wrist in vain?

The evidence of just how thoughtful he was was again there when, having gone up the stairs and into her room, Phinn discovered that someone had been in there.

She stood stock still and just stared. The small round table that had been by the antique gold chaise longue had been removed. In its place, and looking every bit as if it belonged there, was the small round table that had been in the drawing room when last she had seen it.

'Grandmother Hawkins' table,' she said softly, and felt a warm glow wash over her. Welcome home, it seemed to be saying. She did not have to guess who had so thoughtfully made the exchange. She knew that it had been Ty Allardyce.

Phinn went to bed liking him again.

CHAPTER FIVE

PHINN sat on the paddock rail around six weeks later, keeping an eye on Ruby, who'd had a bout of being unwell, and reflecting on how Broadlands Hall now seemed to be quite like home. She knew more of the layout now. Knew where Ty's study was—the place where he always spent some time when he was there.

Most of the rooms had been smartened up, some replastered and redecorated. The room next for redecoration was the music room—the room in which she had often sat listening with Mr Caldicott while her father played on his grand piano. The music room door was occasionally left open, when either Wendy or Valerie, who came up from the village to clean, were in there, giving the room a dusting and an airing. Apparently the piano had been left behind when all Mr Caldicott's other furniture had been removed. Presumably Ty had come to some arrangement with him about it.

Phinn patted Ruby's neck and talked nothings to her while at the same time she reminded herself that she must not allow herself to become too comfortable here. In another four or so months, probably sooner if she were to get anything established for Ruby, she would have to begin looking for a new home for the two of them.

But meantime how good it was to not have that worry

hanging over her head as being immediate. What was imme-diate, however, was the vet's bill that was mounting up. Last month's pay cheque had already gone, and the cheque Ty had left on Grandmother Hawkins' table for her to find a couple of weeks ago was mostly owed to Kit Peverill.

'Don't worry about it,' Kit had told her when she had settled his last veterinary bill. 'There's no rush. Pay me as you can.'

He was kind, was Kit, and, having assumed she had come to the Hall to work in the estate office, he had called to see Ruby as soon as he could when Phinn had phoned. She could not bear to think of Ruby in pain, but Kit had assured her that, though Ruby suffered some discomfort, she was not in actual pain, and that hopefully her sudden loss of appetite would pick up again.

Kit had been kind enough to organise some special food for Ruby, and to Phinn's surprise Geraldine Walton had arrived one day with a load of straw. Ash had been off on one of his 'walkabouts' that day. But soon after that Geraldine had—again to Phinn's surprise—telephoned to say she had a surfeit of hay, and that if Ash was available perhaps he would drive over in the pick-up and collect it.

Having discovered that Ash was at his best when occupied, Phinn had asked him if he would mind. 'Can't you manage without it?' he had enquired, clearly reluctant.

'Yes, of course I can,' she'd replied with a smile. 'I shouldn't have asked you.'

He had been immediately contrite. 'Yes, you should. Sorry, Phinn, I'm not fit company these days. Of course I'll go.' Muttering, 'With luck I shall miss seeing the wretched woman,' he went on his way.

From that Phinn gleaned that it was not so much the errand he was objecting to, but the fact that he did not want any contact with the owner of the riding school and stables. Which gave her cause to wonder if it was just that he had taken an aversion to Geraldine. Or was he, despite himself, attracted to her and a little afraid of her because of what another woman with her colouring had done to him?

Phinn had kept him company as much as she could, though very often she knew that he wanted to be on his own. At other times she had walked miles with him all over the estate lands.

She had talked with him, stayed silent when need be, and when he had mentioned that he quite liked drawing she had several times taken him sketching down by the trout stream. Which had been a little painful to her, because it was there that her father had taught her to sketch.

She had overcome her sadness of spirit when it had seemed to her that Ash appeared to be less stressful and a shade more content when he lost himself as he concentrated on the sketch he was creating.

But Ash was very often quite down, so that sometimes she would wonder if her being there made any difference to him at all. A point she had put to Ty only a week ago. Cutting her nose off it might have been, had he agreed with her and suggested that he would not hold her to their six-month agreement. But it was nothing of the sort!

'Of course you've made a difference,' Ty assured her. 'Apart from the fact I feel I can get back to my work without being too concerned over him, there is a definite improvement from the way he was.'

'You're sure?'

'I'm sure,' he replied, and had meant it. 'Surely you've noticed that he's taking more of an interest in the estate these days? He was telling me on the phone only the other day how you had both met with some forester—Sam...?'

'Sam Turner,' she filled in. 'I was at school with his son Sammy. Sammy's followed in his father's footsteps.' And then, getting carried away, 'Ash and I walked the whole of

Pixie End Wood with Sam and Sammy...' She halted. 'But you probably know that from Ash.'

Ty hadn't answered that, but asked, 'Is there anybody you don't know?'

For the weirdest moment she felt like saying, *I don't know you.* Weird or what? Anybody would think that she *wanted* to know him—better. 'I was brung up around here,' she replied impishly—and felt Ty's steady grey glance on her.

'And a more fully rounded "brung-up" female I've never met,' he commented quietly.

'If I could decide whether that was a compliment or not, I might thank you for it,' she replied.

'It's a compliment,' he informed her, and she had gone about her business wondering about the other women of his acquaintance.

By 'fully rounded' she knew he had not been talking about her figure—which if anything, save for a bosom to be proud of, she had always thought a little on the lean side. So were his London and 'other capitals' women not so generally 'fully rounded'? And was being 'fully rounded' a good thing, or a bad thing? Phinn had given it up when she'd recalled that he had said that it was a compliment.

But now, sitting on the rail mulling over the events of these past weeks, she reflected that Ty, having employed her so that he could go about his business, seemed to come home to Broadlands far more frequently than she had thought he would. Though it was true that here it was Friday, and he had not been home at all this week.

Phinn felt the most peculiar sensation in her insides as she wondered, today being Friday, if Ty would come home to-night? Perhaps he might stay the whole weekend? He didn't always. *Some filly up in London*, her father would have said.

But she did not want to think about Ty and his London fillies. Phinn titled her head a fraction and looked to Ruby, who was watching her. 'Hello, my darling Rubes,' she said softly, and asked, 'What do you say to an apple if I ask Mrs Starkey for one?'

Mrs Starkey was continuing to mother her, and Phinn had to admit she did not object to it. Occasionally she would sit and share a pot of tea with the housekeeper, and Phinn would enquire after Mrs Starkey's son, John, and hear of his latest doings, and then go on to talk of the various other people Phinn had grown up knowing.

Bearing in mind her own mother had taken up golf, and was more often out than in, Phinn *had* made contact with her to let her know of her move. After her mother's third-degree questioning Phinn had ended the call with her mother's blessing.

About to leave her perch and go in search of an apple for Ruby, Phinn just then heard the sound of a car coming up the drive and recognised Kit Peverill's vehicle. She had asked him to come and look Ruby over.

Ruby wasn't too sure about him, but was too timid by nature to raise any strong objections. Instead she sidled up to Phinn and stayed close when he had finished with her.

'She'll do,' he pronounced.

'She's better!' Phinn exclaimed in relief.

'She's never going to be better, Phinn,' Kit replied gently. 'You know that. But she's over this last little upset.'

Phinn looked down at her feet to hide the pain in her eyes. 'Thank you for being so attentive,' she murmured, and, leaving Ruby, walked to his vehicle with him to collect some medication he had mentioned.

'It's always a pleasure to see you, Phinn,' he commented, which took her out of her stride a little, because he had never said anything like it before. Indeed, she had always supposed him to be a tiny bit shy, more of an animal person than a people person. But she was to discover that, while shy, he was not so shy as she had imagined. And that he quite liked people too as well as animals, when he coughed, and followed up with, 'Er—in fact, I've been meaning to ask you—er—how do you feel about coming out with me one night—say, tomorrow night?'

Phinn kept her eyes on the path in front while she considered what he had said. 'Um…' She just hadn't thought of him in a 'date' situation, only a 'vet' situation. 'We—I'm…' Her thoughts were a bit muddled up, but she was thinking more about how long she would want to leave Ruby than of any enjoyment she might find if she dated this rather pleasant man.

'Look, why not give me a ring? I know you won't want to be away from Ruby for too long, but we could have a quick bite over at the Kings Arms in Little Thornby.'

Phinn was on the point of agreeing to go out with him, but something held her back. Perhaps she would go if Ty came home this weekend. Surely she was not expected to stay home being a companion to Ash if Ty was there to keep him company?

'*Can* I give you a ring?' she asked.

After Kit had gone, Phinn thought it time she attended to her duties, and went looking for Ash. The sound of someone busy with a hammer attracted her towards the pool, and she headed in that direction where, to her amazement, she found Ash on the far side, hammering a large signpost into the ground. In bold red the sign proclaimed 'DANGER. KEEP OUT. TREACHEROUS WATER'. Close by was another post, from which hung a lifebelt.

Ash raised his head and saw her. 'Thought I was useless, didn't you?' he called, but seemed the happiest she had seen him since her cousin had done a brilliant job of flattening him.

What Phinn thought was that he was an extremely bruised man, who loved well, but not too wisely, and was paying for it.

'I think you're gorgeous,' she called back with a laugh, and felt a true affection for him. Had she had a brother, she would have liked one just like Ash.

Ash grinned, and for the first time Phinn saw that perhaps her being there *was* making a bit of a difference. Perhaps Ash was starting to heal. Phinn went to get Ruby an apple.

It started to rain after lunch, and although Ruby did not mind the rain, it was heavy enough for Phinn to not want to risk it for her. After stabling her she went indoors, and was coming down the stairs after changing out of damp clothes when the phone in the hall rang.

Phinn had spotted Mrs Starkey driving off in her car about fifteen minutes ago, and, with Ash nowhere to be seen, she picked up the phone with a peculiar sort of hope in her heart that the caller would not be Ty, ringing to say that he wouldn't be home this weekend.

An odd sort of relief entered her soul when the caller was not Ty but Geraldine Walton again, with an offer of more straw. 'I'm running out of space under cover here, so if Ash could pop over he'd be doing me something of a favour,' Geraldine added.

'It's very good of you think of me,' Phinn replied, feeling for certain now that Ash was more the cause for the call than the fact that Geraldine had more straw than she knew what to do with. Geraldine had said not one word about having surplus stocks when she had wandered over yesterday to settle what she owed her! 'Ash isn't around just now. But I'd be glad of the straw,' she accepted.

Phinn was about to go looking for Ash, and found she did not have to when he came crashing in through the front door. 'It's bucketing down out there!' he exclaimed, shaking rain from his arms.

'You don't fancy going out again?'

'Need something?' he enquired, at once willing to go on an errand. He hadn't heard what the errand was yet!

'Geraldine Walton has more straw…' Phinn did not have to say more. Though this time Ash did not seem quite as reluctant as he had before.

'I'll wait for this to give over first,' he said, and, as she herself had done, he went up to change.

The house seemed so quiet when, a half-hour later, keys to the pick-up in hand, Ash left for Geraldine Walton's stables.

Feeling restless suddenly—even Mrs Starkey was out— Phinn was about to go and have a chat to Ruby when, as she was walking past, she saw that the music room door was again open. Either Wendy or Valerie must have left it ajar.

About to close the door and walk on by, Phinn, with her hand on the door handle, found she was hesitating. She had nowhere near the natural talent her father had had for the piano, but he had instructed her well.

It was an age since she had last played. An age since she had last wanted to play. Phinn pushed the door open wider and took a few steps into the room.

She took a few more steps, and a few more, and was then looking down at the piano keys—the lid having been left open because that was best for the piano.

The keys invited. She stretched out a hand and played one note—and then another. And as she stood there she could almost hear her father say, 'Come on, kiddo, let's murder a little Mozart.'

A sob caught the back of her throat. She coughed away the weakness, but felt drawn to sit down on the piano stool. And that was all it took.

She was rusty from lack of practice, but the notes were there— remembered. Her father had loved Mozart. She played Mozart in his memory, remembering the good times they had shared, remembering his laughter. Oh, how he'd loved to laugh…

How long she sat there, 'murdering' Mozart's Concerto Number Twenty-Three, Phinn had no idea. Nor did she have any idea quite when memories of her father started to merge with thoughts of Ty Allardyce.

Nor, when she had just come to the end of the adagio, did she know how long Ty Allardyce had been standing there, watching her. For she felt rather than saw him, and looked up, startled. And then she was startled *and* totally confused. She took her hands from the keys immediately.

'How long have you been standing there?' she gasped, feeling choked suddenly.

'Long enough to know you're a sensitive soul with a splendid touch. And a talent you have been keeping very well hidden.'

She abruptly stood up and, feeling highly emotional just then, moved away from the piano. 'It needs tuning!' she said, purely because she was otherwise bereft of words. She made for the door, but had to halt when Ty blocked her way. 'I'm sorry,' she apologized, for using the instrument. 'You don't mind…?' Her all at once husky voice trailed away, words still defeating her.

'Don't be sorry. I didn't know you could play.' He seemed slightly staggered by his discovery. But he collected himself to tell her, 'Out of tune or not—that was quite beautiful.'

Tall and dark, he looked down at her, still blocking her way. 'I—thought everyone was out…' she began, but he was stretching out a hand to her cheek.

'What's this?' he asked gently, looking down into the deep blue of her eyes. Then, so tenderly she could scarcely believe it, Ty touched her skin and wiped away a stray tear that had rolled down the side of her face uninvited by her. And Phinn at that moment felt too utterly mesmerised to move. Who would have suspected him of such tenderness? 'Sad memories?' he asked softly.

'I—haven't played since my father died,' she replied, her voice still holding that husky note.

'You're still mourning him,' Ty stated.

'We were close. But it's getting better,' she said, and for the first time she felt that it really was.

'Oh, come here,' Ty murmured and, taking a hold of her, he pulled her into his arms. 'I think it's high time someone gave you a hug,' he voiced from above her head.

And, most peculiarly, Phinn found that she was snuggling into his hold and truly liking the feel of his broad manly chest against her face. But she stirred against him. She did not want to move, but this could not be right.

'You've come home for some peace and tranquillity,' she began. 'Not to...' She pulled back from him. 'I'm all right now,' she said.

Ty let her go and stepped back, his grey eyes searching her face. She smiled up at him, to prove that she was indeed all right, and he smiled back. 'If I promise to get the piano tuned, will you promise to come in here and play whenever you want to—regardless of who's in and who's out?' Phinn stared at him numbly, and he smiled and made her feel weepy again, when he assured her, 'This is your home now.'

Too full suddenly to say a word, Phinn quickly went by him—out from the music room, along the hall, and straight up the stairs to her room. She had acknowledged that Ty did strange things to her long before she got there.

Collapsing onto the bedroom chair, she found her thoughts were not of her father, as they so often had been, but of Ty Allardyce and the complex man he was.

After having been ready at one time to throw her off his lands, he was now telling her that this, Broadlands Hall, was her home! Obviously he was only referring to it being her temporary home, but still the same, Ty just saying what he had had the effect of making her feel less rootless—albeit only temporarily.

She remembered that oh, so tender touch to her cheek, remembered the gentle way he had held her in his arms, and, most oddly, felt that she wanted to be back in his arms, back being held by him again.

But if he was a complex man, what about her? Only then did she realise how overwhelmingly pleased she was that he was home!

Which—the fact that it pleased her to know he was there—made it seem somewhat illogical to her that she felt reluctant to go down and see him again. Shy? Her? Never! She glanced at her watch. His watch. And felt decidedly not herself. What on earth was the man doing to her, for goodness' sake?

Nothing! Nothing at all, she told herself stoutly. Grief, it was just that, having been around men pretty much all her life—her father's friends, mainly—she had never met any man quite like Tyrell Allardyce.

Still the same, since he was home to keep his brother company—if Ash was back—Phinn saw no good reason to go down.

She did, however, leave her room briefly to go and check on Ruby. But she returned to her room and, when clothes had never particularly bothered her before—what she wore being immaterial so long as it was clean and respectable—she spent some time wondering if she should perhaps put on a dress for a change.

Ten minutes later, having dithered on the yes or no question for more than long enough, Phinn decided she must be going mental! Smart trousers and a top had been good enough all this week. Why on earth would she want to wear a dress just because Ty was home?

At seven twenty-five, wearing the smart trousers and a top, Phinn went down the stairs to the drawing room, where the two brothers were in idle conversation.

Her glance went straight to Ty, who looked across the moment she came in. He made no mention of her piano-playing activities, and she was grateful for his sensitivity there.

'Would you like something to drink, Phinn?' he enquired

courteously. She shook her head. She wasn't shy; she knew that she wasn't. She just felt not herself somehow. 'Then perhaps we'd better go and see what Mrs Starkey has in store for us,' he said with a smile.

What Mrs Starkey had in store, after a superb cheese soufflé starter, was trout with almonds as a main course—which gave Ash cause to remark to his brother, 'Phinn took me fly-fishing yesterday.' Lack of space had dictated that her father's piano had to go, but Phinn had been unable to part with his fishing equipment. 'You know—the trout stream I sketched? It's hidden behind Long Meadow,' Ash continued.

'Long Meadow?' Ty queried, with a glance to Phinn.

'Been there years,' she obliged.

'You should see Phinn cast a line!' Ash went on. And then reported, 'She's promised to teach me to tie a fly.'

Ty's gaze was on her again, with that expression on his face that she was getting to know. 'Is there nothing you cannot do?' he asked lightly.

'Heaps of things,' she replied, and felt obliged to mention, since this clever man must know full well that her casting skills had been learned while trespassing in waters that belonged to the estate, 'Old Mr Caldicott used to appreciate the odd trout.'

Ty looked from her to the trout on his plate. 'You caught these yesterday?'

But even while she was shaking her head, Ash was chipping in. 'Not Phinn. Me. Phinn went all girly on me and put her catch back. Though...' Ash looked down at his own plate '...I don't remember mine being this big.'

'You'll never make a fisherman, Ash,' Phinn butted in, aware that all the fishermen *she* knew exaggerated sublimely. She guessed that Mrs Starkey's errand that afternoon had included a visit to the fishmonger's in town.

And while Ash was grinning, Ty asked him what else he

had been up to that week. 'Walked a lot. Fished a lot,' Ash answered. 'Ran an errand for Phinn. Oh, and prior to the specialists you arranged getting here to survey and check out the Dark Pool, I took delivery of that danger notice we talked about and hammered it in. Looks all right too—even though apart from us it's only trespassers that are likely to see it.'

Ty looked to Phinn, and as her lips twitched on recalling the way he had threatened to have her summonsed for trespassing, his rather pleasant-shaped mouth picked up too, and there seemed to be only the two of them there, in a kind of small, intimate moment between them.

And then Ash was going on. 'Phinn thinks I'm gorgeous, by the way.'

Phinn shared a grin with Ash, feeling just then that they had become firm friends. But, happening to glance back at Ty, she saw that he was suddenly looking more hostile, if anything. Certain then that she had imagined any kind of an intimate moment with him, she could only wonder what she had done wrong now.

For courtesy's sake, in front of Ash, she pretended that she was unaffected whichever way Ty looked at her, or however hostile he was. What had happened to the tender, understanding man of that afternoon?

Phinn ate her way through the rest of her meal, but could not wait to be able to leave the dining room. The moment the meal was at an end, she was getting to her feet.

'If you'll excuse me?' she said politely to no one in particular. 'I'll go along and check on Ruby.' Both men were on their feet too. Phinn did not wait to find out whether they objected or not.

Having been stewed up inside for the last half-hour, Phinn calmed down as she tended to Ruby. And the calmer she became, gradually she began to see what Ty's hostile look had been all about. Ash, because of her cousin, had got himself into quite a state. Ty, seeing her and Ash getting on so well—and for all his previous opinion that his brother was so ensnared by her cousin that other women did not exist—must now be afraid that another of the Hawkins clan was getting to him. There was no other explanation for that hostile look.

Well, he need not worry. She and Ash were friends and nothing more. And, conscious of how concerned Ty had been, and probably still was, about Ash, she had one very good way of putting him straight.

Though before she could go and see him she spotted Ruby's ears pricking up, and had a fair idea then that she wouldn't have to wait that long.

Nor did she. And as Ty stepped into the stable, before she could say anything, he got in first. 'I wanted a word with you.'

For one dreadful moment Phinn thought he was going to ask her to leave. But even with that sinking feeling in the pit of her stomach, pride stormed in to make her aggressive. 'I didn't do it—whatever it was!' she stated, showing a fair degree of hostility of her own.

Ty stared at her in some surprise. 'Heaven help us!' he grunted. 'Do you always meet trouble halfway?'

'I'm in trouble?' she questioned belligerently.

'You will be if you don't shut up and let me get a word in!'

She opened her mouth, and then closed it. Then opened it again to tell him, 'Whatever it is, don't raise your voice and frighten my horse!'

'Oh, God, you're priceless,' Ty muttered, and, putting his hand into his trouser pocket, he pulled out something and handed it to her. 'Here,' he said, 'I got you this.'

Having taken it from him, Phinn looked and was stunned at what he had given her. 'A watch!' she gasped. And not just any old watch, but a most beautiful watch!

'The one you have on is much too big for your delicate wrist,' he commented.

But just then Phinn suddenly noticed the maker's name, and warm colour rushed to her face. 'You got this especially for me?' she questioned—it must have cost a mint! Hurriedly she thrust it back at him. 'No, thank you,' she told him primly.

'No?' He seemed quite taken out of his stride—as if it had never occurred to him that she would not accept it. 'What do you mean, no?' he questioned shortly.

'It's too expensive!'

'Don't be ridiculous!' he rapped.

And that infuriated her. 'Don't you call me ridiculous!' she hissed, even in her fury mindful of Ruby. 'My watch—if that's meant to be a replacement—cost only about forty pounds. I wouldn't even hazard a guess at the price you paid for that one.' And, as Ty continued to stare at her, 'If you want this one back—' she began, starting to undo the clasp.

Ty's hand coming to hers to stay her action caused a tingle to shoot through her body. 'Keep it on,' he ordered. Then all at once his tough expression changed. 'Have I offended you, Phinn?' he asked softly.

And just then, right at that very moment, Phinn knew—quite absurdly—that she was in love with him. Just like that she knew.

Again, from the pure emotion of the moment, she went red. Though she somehow managed to keep her head to tell him, 'Right is right and wrong is wrong. And that—' indicating the watch in his hand '—is wrong.'

Ty studied her for long silent moments. Then, slipping the watch back into his pocket, 'I don't think I've ever met anyone with quite such high morals as you,' he stated.

'Then you've been mixing with totally the wrong company,' she replied with an impish grin, though was uncertain that she wanted to be considered too much of a goody-goody. Although, on thinking about it, to have trespassed quite happily all over his land without the smallest compunction did, she felt, rather tarnish her goody-goody halo a little bit. 'Anyhow, I rather wanted to have a word with you too.' She looked from him, scared for a moment that this new love she felt for him might somehow be visible to him.

'What's wrong?' he asked sharply.

'Nothing's wrong!' she snapped back, moving away from Ruby—if they were going to have a row, she would prefer that her Rubes, so sensitive to atmosphere, did not know about it. 'The thing is,' she went on more calmly—time now to let him know that *this* Hawkins wasn't after his brother, or him either for that matter, time to let him know that she had other fish to fry. 'Er…' How to get started? 'Will you be here tomorrow night?' She said it the only way she could: bluntly.

Ty eyed her for a couple of solid seconds. 'You're asking me for a date?' he enquired, his expression completely serious.

Phinn rolled her eyes heavenward. 'It's not your birthday!' she answered snappily but then, probably because a date with Ty sounded like just so much bliss, 'I have other irons in the fire,' she informed him snootily. 'Kit, the vet, has asked me out tomorrow night.'

'The vet? He's been here?'

'Several times, actually. Ruby has been unwell.'

'She's better now?' he asked tersely.

Phinn declined to go into details of the anxiety of it all, but agreed that Ruby was well again. 'So, given that I wouldn't want to leave her for too long, I presume I'm allowed some time off—if you're at home?'

Ty studied her as though he did not care very much for this conversation. But then suddenly he smiled. It was a silky kind of smile; one she had no belief in!

And she knew that she was right not to have belief in it when, his voice as silky as his smile, he said, 'My dear Miss Hawkins, how could you have forgotten?'

She quickly racked her brains, but could think of nothing she had forgotten. 'Forgotten what?'

'That you can't possibly go out with him.'

'Why can't I?' she demanded belligerently.

He smiled again. Love him she might, but she still wanted to swipe that smile off his face. 'How can you go out with another man,' he enquired pleasantly, 'when you know full well that you're supposed to be my girlfriend?'

For a stunned couple of seconds, Phinn stared at him, speechless. And then it was that she remembered that Ty did not want Ash to know that the real reason she was there was to keep him company, and that she had gone along with that. She had also agreed that Ash had enough of a burden weighing on him, and had agreed too, she supposed, to let Ash believe what he obviously believed—that she was there more as Ty's friend than his. In fact his girlfriend—would-be—sort of.

In actual fact, now she came to think of it, she did not feel too put out that her dating facility had been curtailed. But she gave Ty a look of disgust for his trouble anyway, and, muttering an old family saying, 'Well, give me a kiss and lend me tuppence!' which was meant to convey her disgust, she turned sharply away from him.

Then nearly died of fright when, spinning her back round to him, Ty replied, 'Anything to oblige,' with a wicked kind of gleam in his eyes. And the next thing Phinn knew Ty had hauled her into his arms and his head was coming down.

Desperately she tried to avoid his lips, but with one hand moving up to the back of her head he held her still. Then his mouth settled over hers and she was lost.

Unhurriedly, he eased her lips apart, and while her heart hammered frantically away inside her, he held her close up against him. And Phinn never wanted it to end.

A discreet kind of cough from the doorway made her jerk

away from Ty. But he still had an arm about her waist as they both turned to see a grinning Ash standing there.

'Sorry to interrupt,' he said, not looking sorry at all, but looking very much like the Ash she had known before her cousin had so unceremoniously dumped him. 'But the vet's been on the phone. I didn't know if it would be important or not, now that Ruby seems better, but I said you would call him back.'

'Oh, thanks, Ash,' Phinn replied, trying to gather her scattered wits. And, needing to be on her own, 'I'll go and call him now,' she added.

But so much for being on her own to sort her feelings out. 'I'll come with you,' Ty offered, and while Ash went on his way, actually whistling 'Love Is in the Air', Phinn left the stable hoping that Ty had no idea of what the tune was.

She was still feeling all of a fluster from Ty's kiss—which she had to admit, reluctantly, that she might have inadvertently invited—when, with Ty still by her side, they reached the house.

They were in the hall and within a yard of the phone when, with Phinn making no attempt to slow her speed, Ty caught a hold of her arm. 'Make the call from here,' he ordered. 'Tell him you're spoken for.'

And bang went her feeling of being all mixed up inside. 'Like blazes, I will!' she erupted, not taking kindly to being so bossed about—after he had kissed her so wonderfully too! If she rang Kit Peverill at all, it would be in the privacy of her room and on her mobile.

But, with Ty still holding her arm, the matter was settled when the phone just then rang. Ty stretched forward and picked it up. 'Allardyce,' he said, and while he listened Phinn was thinking it might be some business call and she could make her escape. 'Phinn's here now,' she heard him say. And then he was handing the phone to her and insisting, 'Tell him.'

Phinn sent him a malevolent look, which bounced straight off him, and took hold of the phone. She guessed the call must be from Kit, and wished Ty Allardyce would clear off because, although he had let go of her arm, he was still standing there, clearly bent on listening to her every word.

'Hello,' she managed pleasantly, after taking a calming breath.

'I hope you don't mind me ringing again, Phinn,' Kit replied, a touch diffidently. 'Only I'm on call, and I thought I'd leave you my on-call number so I wouldn't miss you when you rang. Er—have you thought any more about tomorrow night?'

She felt uncomfortable, and that feeling was not helped when Ty Allardyce seemed immune to her killing looks. 'The thing is, Kit…' she began. 'I—um—I'm sorry.'

'You can't make it?' He sounded disappointed. 'Perhaps some other time? If…'

'Well, to be honest—' since the deed had to be done, she now wanted it done and out of the way '—your invitation— er—sort of caught me on the wrong foot. That is—I've just— er—started seeing someone.' There—it was done.

'Oh,' Kit mumbled. 'Oh, all right.' And, 'Er—if it doesn't work out…'

'Of course,' she replied, but could not help but feel awful, even if she now knew that she did not want to date Kit. But, as she put the phone down, it did not make her any less cross with Ty Allardyce. 'Satisfied?' she asked him waspishly.

And he smiled, a more genuine smile this time. 'Don't be mad at me, Phinnie,' he said charmingly. 'You know he doesn't mean anything to you.'

'How do I know?' Smile or no smile she was at her belligerent best. 'We—Kit and I—we might have been—er—made for each other.'

But Ty was shaking his head. 'I kissed you, Phinn. But you kissed me back.' And, as warm colour stained her cheeks, 'You wouldn't have done that had the vet been in there with so much as half a chance.'

Phinn stared at him open-mouthed. 'How did you get to know so much about women?' she exclaimed in disgust. But then, as jealousy nipped for the first time ever in her life, 'Don't tell me!' she ordered. 'I don't want to know!' And with that she turned about and stormed angrily away.

But the truth of the matter was, he was right. He thought she had high morals, and while she did not know about that, what she *did* know was that he was right in that she would not have returned his kiss had she felt anything at all for Kit Peverill. More, having fallen in love with Ty Allardyce, she knew without doubt that the idea of being in any man's arms other than his was absolutely abhorrent to her.

Now, why had she gone and fallen in love with him? Of all the idiotic things to do, wasn't that the cruncher? Kiss her he might—if invited. And she could not deny her inviting words were probably enough for any red-blooded male—be she his pretend girlfriend or no. But when it came to the love stakes idiotic was what it truly was. Because worldly, sophisticated men like Tyrell Allardyce just did not fall in love with lippy, trespassing 'village locals' like her.

Phinn returned to the stable to chat to Ruby. She had only just discovered her feelings for Ty, but one way and another she was finding it all very disheartening.

Though, whatever else happened during the remainder of her time at Broadlands, all Phinn knew—with Ty Allardyce knowing so very much about women—was that she was going to have to keep her feelings for him extremely well hidden!

CHAPTER SIX

SATURDAY began with a miserable wet dawn, but Phinn could not be down. She'd had a restless night, and awoke to know that her love for Ty was no figment of her imagination. It was still there this morning and, while she would take great care that he would never know of it, it gave her a feeling of joy to know that he was here, at home.

She did not want to think of how it would be when he went back to London, but decided that for the moment she would just enjoy knowing that he was sleeping under the same roof.

Phinn showered and dressed early and, with her hair pulled back in a band, slipped quietly out of the house.

It was while she was talking to Ruby that Phinn realised she must have begun to fall in love with Ty as far back as when he had offered them a home. Incredible as it seemed, it must have been then. She clearly recalled thinking then that there was something not right about it somewhere. Now she knew what it was—some sixth sense had been trying to warn her that before too long she was going to get hurt.

Too late now to do anything about it. She was in love with him, and that love was here to stay. She knew that.

When Phinn went back to the house, both Ty and Ash were at breakfast. All at once feeling a sudden eagerness to see Ty again, she hastened up the stairs to wash and tidy signs of the stable from her before going quickly down again.

'Ty wants to take a walk around the estate. Coming with us?' Ash asked.

Normally she would have liked nothing better. But, sensitive to the two brothers, she thought that perhaps they might need some brotherly time together, and they would probably talk more easily if she were not there.

'I've a date with...' Pure wickedness made her look at Ty—there was a glint in his eyes that said he was listening, and was daring her to have a date with the vet. 'With a pitchfork, a wheelbarrow and, by special request, Jimmie Starkey's compost heap.'

'Whatever turns you on,' Ash replied, and, with a smile, 'If you prefer mucking out the stable to a morning spent in fascinating company...'

Phinn grinned at him, affection for him in her look, and real pleasure in her heart as she noticed how his appetite had started to pick up. With luck that twenty or so pounds he had lost would soon be put back on again.

'Did you sleep well?' Ty butted in sharply.

Taken by surprise, Phinn turned to him, startled. 'Do I look haggard?' she queried.

One sleepless night and she looked a wreck!

His answer was to study her for all of one full minute. And, just when she was thinking that she was going to go red at any second, 'You look quite beautiful,' he answered, so entirely unexpectedly and sounding so much as if he meant it, that she did blush.

She recovered quickly, however, and, having realised that his remark had to be because Ash was there, and that Ty was merely playing his role of being interested in her, she told him lightly, 'I'm still not coming with you.'

Up in her room after breakfast, she went and stared at her face in the mirror. She wanted to be beautiful. She wanted Ty to think she was beautiful. But did a straight nose, wide and quite nice delphinium-blue eyes, eyebrows that were a shade darker than her strawberry-blonde hair, a dainty chin and a fairly nice forehead—oh, and a complexion that, yes, had been remarked on in the past as 'quite something'—constitute beauty? Her phone rang and put an end to her daydreaming.

It was her mother, her morning's golf having been cancelled because Clive had a heavy cold. 'How are things, darling? And how's Ruby?' It was good to chat to her mother, and they talked for some while, with her mother ending, 'When are we going to see you?'

Promising to try and pay them a visit soon, Phinn rang off, reflecting that her mother had a very different life now from the one she had had with her father. But this wasn't getting Ruby's stable sorted.

The early-morning rain had cleared when, changed into old jeans and a tee shirt, Phinn turned Ruby out into the paddock and went back to the stable. Before she could start work, though, Ty Allardyce appeared. How she loved him! Her heart raced. How he must never know.

'The weather's cleared for your walk,' she offered, friendly, polite—that was the way. But, forget it. Ty, it seemed, had come looking for a fight.

'Have you been in touch with Peverill?' he questioned bluntly, coming to stand but a yard from her. What happened to *You look quite beautiful*? Phinn thought.

'Since my telephone conversation with him last night, you mean?'

Ty gave her an impatient look. 'I passed your room—you were on the phone with someone.'

What big ears you have! For one delicious moment, Phinn had the weird notion that Ty had sounded jealous. See where falling in love got you—it made you weird in the head! All he was bothered about was the thought that she might blow their cover by going out with the vet after all.

Despite her inner turmoil, Phinn smiled at him sweetly. 'You don't really mind if I chat on the phone to my mother occasionally? It's ages since I last saw her.'

Ty's annoyed look instantly fell away. 'I've been a brute again, haven't I?' He did not expect an answer.

He got one anyway. 'You can't help it. It's your nature,' Phinn replied—and just had to laugh. She didn't believe it for a moment. What *was* his nature was a big brother's need to look out for his younger brother—and if that included taking her to task if he thought she was going to put a spoke in the wheel of the progress he had made so far, he would.

But Ty was unoffended by her remark, and actually seemed amused by it. Then, taking on board what she had just said about not having seen her mother for ages, and remembering she had sold her car, he was serious as he suggested, 'There are several vehicles here if you'd like to go and visit your mother.' And, as an afterthought, 'I'll take you to see her myself, if you prefer.'

'Wouldn't dream of it,' Phinn replied, thinking again what a complex man he was. He had come to see her ready to sort her out, and here he was offering to spend some of his precious weekend taking her family visiting!

'Or why not invite her and her husband here for a meal? Your mother could see where—'

Phinn stopped him right there. 'Do you know, Ty,' she butted in, 'when you forget to be a brute, you sometimes surprise me by being really, really nice?'

He looked taken aback. But then, as if noting from her solemn-eyed expression that she was being sincere, his tone changed when he quietly stated, 'You do realise that if you carry on in that vein, you're in serious danger of being kissed again.'

Oh, my, how he could make her heart race! Phinn teetered on the brink of saying, *Promises, promises*—but instinctively knew that such a remark was bound to guarantee that Ty *would* kiss her. And, while heart and soul she would welcome his kisses, she knew that that way lay danger: danger of Ty, with his experience.

Which was why she forced herself to take a step away from him. 'One kiss in twenty-four hours is more than enough for us village locals,' she told him primly.

His lips twitched. 'You're never going to let me forget that "village locals" comment, are you?'

'Not if I still know you when you're a hundred,' she replied cheerfully. And offered nicely, 'If you want to help I'm sure I can rustle up another pitchfork from somewhere.'

He looked amused. 'You certainly know how to say good-bye to a man,' he said, declining her offer, and went.

After that, the day seemed to fly by. Ty and Ash came back from their inspection of the estate, with Ty approving of Sam Turner's suggestions for keeping Pixie End Wood healthy.

After a quick lunch he said he had arranged to call in at Yew Tree Farm. 'Anyone like to come?' he asked.

'You and Phinn go,' Ash suggested. 'If Phinn will loan me her rods, I fancy having another go at casting.'

'Oh, I don't—' Phinn began. Ash was welcome to borrow her fishing equipment, but Ty wouldn't want her with him when he went to call on his tenants at Yew Tree Farm.

'That's fine,' Ty cut in. 'See you in half an hour then, Phinn.'

She opened her mouth to protest, saw Ty was looking at her with something of a stern expression, and, probably because deep down she wanted to spend some time with him, 'Off-hand, I can't think of anything I'd rather do,' she remarked.

Of course Ty thought she was being saucy, but she did not care. Did not care either that he would probably just as soon go on his own. But if he wanted Ash to think that they were more friendly than they were, who was she to argue?

'Ruby all right?' Ty queried when, thirty-five minutes later, with Ash in possession of her father's fishing equipment, Phinn sat beside Ty in his car and they set off.

Ruby, in Phinn's view, was a nice safe topic. 'She's feeling great today,' she replied happily.

'But doesn't always?'

'Poor love, she's getting on a bit. Sometimes she's fine for weeks on end, but just lately—well, she's had more bad days than good.'

'And that's where the vet comes in?'

Not so safe a topic. 'Kit has been brilliant.' She gave the vet his due. 'Most attentive.'

'I'll bet,' Ty muttered. Then, plainly not interested in the vet, 'Tell me about Phinn Hawkins,' he requested.

'You know everything.'

'I very much doubt that,' he replied.

'What do you want to know?'

'You could start by telling me your first name?' he suggested.

And have him laugh his socks off? Not likely! 'You know my first name.'

'Phinn doesn't begin with a "D",' he countered. She wondered how on earth he knew that her first name began with a "D". 'Your father's initials were "E.H." The only other initials carved into the underside of Grandmother Hawkins' table are "D.H".'

'You checked?' she asked, startled.

'I spotted the initials when I purchased the table, obviously. Since I was the one who upended it to take it to your room, I couldn't very well miss seeing them again.'

'I never did thank you for that lovely gesture. I did—do—appreciate it.'

'So, what does the "D" stand for?' Stubbornly, she refused to answer. 'You're not going to deny the "D" is yours, I hope?'

'So, about me. I was born at Honeysuckle Farm and was adored by my parents and grandparents. Because my mother was quite poorly after having me—some complication or other—my father looked after me, and he never stopped even when she was well again.'

'As he adored you, you in turn adored him?' Ty put in.

'Absolutely! He was wonderful. A gifted pianist. A…'

'It was he who taught you to play?'

'Yes.' She nodded, remembering those hours at the piano. 'Just as he taught me so many other things.'

'Go on,' Ty urged, when she drifted off with her thoughts for a second or two.

'You can't possibly be interested.'

'I wouldn't have asked had I not been interested,' he replied—a touch sharply, she felt. She mustn't go reading into it that he might be interested in any personal way in Phinn Hawkins. 'What "many other things" did he teach you?'

'Apart from how to trespass all over Broadlands?'

'He taught that one well,' Ty commented—but she sensed amusement rather than censure in his tone.

'He also taught me to respect the property I was trespassing on. Not to fish out of season, where to swim and where not to swim.'

'How to perform a flat-out racing dive?'

'We owe that one to him,' she murmured.

'That alone forgives him anything he ever did wrong,' Ty said quietly, and they both knew they were talking of her rescue dive. 'The courage it took to do it, though, was all your own,' he added.

But Phinn loved him, and did not want him to relive a time when he might have lost his beloved brother in what was a very heart-tearing memory for him. 'Anyhow,' she said brightly, 'having bought me many books he thought I should be reading, and having many times taken me out of school when he thought they were neglecting areas they should be teaching me, he would take me round museums and art galleries. We went everywhere—concerts, opera... And when town got too much we would come home and walk through the woods, and he would teach me about trees and animals. Teach me how to sketch, how to fish, tie a fly and appreciate Mozart.' She smiled as she confessed, 'I learned by myself how to take a swig of my father's beer down at the pub without pulling a face at the foul taste.' Her smile became a light laugh as she added, 'I supposed I learned by myself too, how to cuss and swear. I was less than four years old, it seems when I apparently came out with a mouthful that nearly sent my grandmother into heart failure and saw my mother banning my father from taking me anywhere near the Cat and Drum.'

There *was* a smile in Ty's voice when he suggested, 'You grew out of cussing very quickly, I take it?'

'In record time, I think you could say—and the ban was lifted,' she answered with a grin. 'And that is more than enough about me. Your turn.'

'Turn?' he queried, as if he had no idea what she meant.

'Oh, don't be mean! I've just talked my head off about me!'

'You can't...'

'Possibly be interested? That's my line! And I am.'

'Interested in me?'

'In a purely reciprocal way,' she replied—she who was avid to know every last little thing about him. 'According to Ash, you're a genius when it comes to business.'

'Business is quite good at the moment,' he replied—rather modestly, Phinn thought.

'You mean it's thriving?'

'It occupies a lot of my time.'

'But you love it?'

'It adds that bit of adrenalin to my day,' he admitted, adding, 'I'm out of the country all of next week.'

Her heart sank. It was being greedy, she knew, but if Ty was going to be out of the country all next week, then there was absolutely no chance whatsoever that he would come down to Broadlands any weekday evening.

'Ash will miss you,' she said, but could easily have substituted her own name.

'He'll be all right,' Ty answered. 'With you here I can safely go away, knowing that he could never have a better guardian.'

Feeling that they were getting away from the subject of him, Phinn was just about to ask him which university he had attended when she suddenly became aware that they were driving through the land farmed by Nesta and Noel Jarvis, the tenants of Yew Tree Farm. And the further they drove on, with flourishing fields on either side of the road, the more the contrast between Yew Tree Farm and Honeysuckle Farm hit her full square. Yew Tree Farm was thriving! The Jarvises must have had the same hard times that Honeysuckle had experienced. But where Honeysuckle had gone under, Yew Tree had somehow survived—had borne the fall in wheat prices, the rising cost of fuel, and had continued to make the farm the success it was today.

Neighbours of Honeysuckle, they had suffered the same vagaries of weather, all the wet summers, and must have endured the same machinery breakdowns, yet—they were thriving!

Phinn was reduced to silence as Ty steered his vehicle into the farmyard. No air of neglect here. No heaps of rusting machinery. Remembering Honeysuckle and its neglected air the last time she had seen it, she did not want to get out of the car. Perhaps she could stay where she was. Ty had said he was merely going to call in—perhaps his business would not take that long.

But, no, he was coming round to the passenger side and opening the door. Already he had a hand on her arm. 'If your business is private…' she suggested.

Ty looked at her, and seemed to guess from her expression that something was amiss, because, 'What is it?' he asked. But before she could tell him both Nesta and Noel Jarvis, having heard their vehicle, had come out to greet them.

Not wanting to cause a fuss, Phinn shook her head at Ty and, with his hand on her arm, stepped from the car. She pinned a smile on her face as Mr and Mrs Jarvis recognised her.

'You know Phinn, of course,' Ty commented as he shook hands with the couple.

'Phinn, my dear, how are you?' Nesta Jarvis asked. They had known Phinn all her life, and had both been at her father's funeral. 'We heard you were working at Broadlands now. How are you getting along?'

'We would be lost without her, Mrs Jarvis,' Ty commented, and enquired of Noel Jarvis, 'Busy time of year for you, I expect?'

They did not overstay their welcome, but while Ty politely refused an offer of refreshments and went into the study with Noel, Phinn stayed and had a cup of tea with Nesta. They passed the time with Nesta enquiring after her mother, and Phinn enquiring after the Jarvises' son and two daughters. The girls had married and moved away, while the son, Gregory, had married and now lived in a farm cottage, working with his father.

Phinn was still in a quiet frame of mind when, having said farewell to the Jarvises, she sat beside Ty on the journey back to the Hall.

Then suddenly Ty was steering the vehicle into a lay-by and pulling up. Phinn turned in her seat to look at him. 'Are you going to share it with me, Phinn?' he asked quietly, seriously.

She could have told him that there was nothing to share, but at the very least she owed him an apology. She swallowed on a knot of emotion, then with a shaky sigh began. 'I hated you when you gave us notice to quit. But you were right. We weren't paying the rent—and the place was a tip.'

'That wasn't your fault,' Ty put in quietly.

But she wasn't having that. 'You asked if there was nothing I couldn't do—well, I well and truly messed up there! I should have made more of an effort, but I didn't. And it's taken going to Yew Tree Farm today and seeing what a well-run farm should look like for me to see it.'

'Don't beat yourself up about it, Phinn,' Ty instructed her seriously. 'You had a home to run. Nobody would have expected you to be out riding a tractor all day.' She still felt she should have done more. Though it was a fact that Ty certainly made her feel better when he asked, 'Would your father have been happy for you to take on *his* work?'

Put like that, no, he would not. Her father might not have shown much interest in running the farm, but she knew he would have taken great exception had she attempted to take over. Her mother had often called her her father's playmate, and Phinn knew she would have taken the fun out of what had been his last days had she said that she had work to do each time he asked her to go somewhere with him. He had disliked it intensely when she had left the farm each day to go to her job at the accountants.

'How do you always know how to say just the right thing?' she asked Ty, and he smiled a gentle smile.

But, as her heart seemed to skip a beat, his smile deepened and he murmured conspiratorially, 'I'll bet Noel Jarvis can't play the piano like your father could.'

Oh, Ty. She loved him so. 'I bet he couldn't have trimmed my Easter bonnet like my dad did either,' she said, and was able to laugh. She loved Ty the more that he did not think her odd, but seemed to *know* that her dad trimming her Easter bonnet had been something rather special.

'All right now?' he asked.

She nodded. 'Yes,' she said. 'And—thank you.' And she felt the world was a wonderful place when, leaning across to her, Ty placed a brief kiss on her cheek.

'Let's go home—and see if Ash has caught any more trout.'

What they did find when they reached the house was that

there was a beat-up old car on the drive. And as they went in Phinn clearly heard what to her was the unmistakable sound of a piano tuner at work.

She stopped dead in her tracks. 'Mr Timmins?' she queried of Ty, who had halted with her.

'Mr Timmins,' he agreed with a grin.

Phinn sailed up to her room. Mr Timmins never worked on Saturday afternoons for *anyone*! But, remembering Ty's wonderful grin, she felt just then that *she* would do anything for Ty too.

All too soon Saturday gave way to Sunday. It was a joy to her that Ty had decided not to leave for London until very early on Monday morning, but to Phinn the hours on Sunday went by in a flash.

That evening after dinner, while she *wanted* to stay in the drawing room, where Ty was, she made herself get to her feet.

'I'm for bed,' she said, to no one in particular. And, because she just had to look at him, 'Have a good trip next week,' she bade Ty.

He stood up and walked to the door with her—purely for Ash's benefit, she knew. 'See you hopefully on Friday,' he murmured when they halted at the door, out of earshot of Ash.

Phinn nodded. 'Bye, you,' she said, and looked up into a pair of steady grey eyes.

'Bye yourself,' he said softly, and, to make her heart go positively wild, he bent down and, otherwise not touching her, gently kissed her on the mouth.

Phinn wheeled away from him without a word. Only when she got to her room and closed the door did she put her fingertips to the lips he had kissed. Oh, my!

It was not the same Broadlands without Ty there. The summer had temporarily disappeared, and it did nothing but rain on Monday. Bearing in mind that Ash still had a tendency to be a bit down occasionally, mainly in the afternoon,

Phinn sought him out and offered to give him a fly-tying lesson.

But on Tuesday *she* was the one who was down. Ruby was ill again. Kit Peverill was as good as ever, and recommended a new medicine for Ruby. New and expensive.

'I'd like her to have it,' Phinn told him, wanting the best for her Rubes, even if she had no idea how she was going to pay for it.

'Don't worry about settling your account straight away,' Kit said kindly, just as if he knew she was near to broke.

But she did worry about it. Before Kit had asked her out, the fact she sometimes owed him money had not unduly bothered her. She'd always known that she would pay him some time. But now that he had asked her out it seemed to make it more of a personal debt to him, somehow. And she did not like it.

By Thursday, however, Ruby was starting to pick up again, her new medication obviously suiting her. Phinn knew then that, whatever the cost, there was no way Ruby was going to stop taking it.

It was raining again at lunchtime, and while on the one hand Phinn was delighted with Ruby's progress, she could not lose that niggle of worry about owing the vet money.

Ash came and found her in the stables, and he did not seem very bright either. Phinn had an idea. It was too wet to take Ash off for a good long walk, but there was somewhere else she could take him.

'If you were very good, Ashley Allardyce, I might think of taking you down to the pub for a pint,' she told him, managing to sound more bright than she felt.

Ash looked at her, considered the proposition and, with not much else happening in his life just then, accepted. 'If you promise to behave yourself, I might come,' he said. And, since they would both be soaked if they walked anywhere very far in the present downpour, 'The pick-up okay?'

The Cat and Drum was full of its usual lunchtime regulars. 'Take a seat over there,' Phinn instructed him. 'I'll get the drinks.'

'No, I'll get them,' Ash insisted.

'Actually, Ash, I rather wanted to have a private word with the landlord.'

'Devious maid,' Ash accused, though he didn't seem to mind that there had been a motive behind her invite to the pub. 'Make mine a pint.'

Telling Bob Quigley that she would like a quick word with him, Phinn delivered Ash his pint and returned to have a discussion with the landlord.

Phinn had finished her discussion with him when, as she half turned, she saw that Ash was deep in conversation with none other than Geraldine Walton!

Far from being the grumpy kind of man he had been with Geraldine when she had first introduced the two, Phinn observed that Ash seemed in no particular hurry to cut short the conversation they were having. In fact, to Phinn's mind, Ash seemed suddenly to be very much lifted from his earlier mood.

In no hurry either to interrupt them, and wondering if Geraldine usually stopped by the Cat at lunchtime or if she had been passing and had recognised the pick-up parked outside, Phinn was glad just then to be accosted by Mickie Yates.

'What are you doing in this iniquitous place, young lady?' he greeted her warmly.

'Mickie!' she exclaimed, and kissed his whiskery cheek.

Chatting with Mickie took up a good five minutes—but Ash and Geraldine were still finding things to talk about. Don't hurt him! Phinn thought, finding protective feelings for Ash rushing to the surface. But then she reminded herself that, while Geraldine could not afford to be a softie and run a successful business, the owner of the riding school and stables was nowhere as hard-hearted and avaricious as her cousin Leanne.

Rather than have Ash look over and think he might be

obliged to come back to her, Phinn stayed turned away from him. Jack Philips, an old friend of her father, came up to her, and then Idris Owen joined in, in to collect fresh supplies to take back to his forge. She could have chatted with them all day.

Eventually a much more cheerful Ash came over to them. When they at last left the pub, he asked if she had seen Geraldine Walton there, and Phinn replied, 'I did, actually. I hope you don't think me rude, but I didn't want to be impolite to my father's old friends and come over.'

'If you'd accepted all the drinks they offered you'd be staggering,' was all he replied.

Ruby continued to make progress, and Kit Peverill visited early on Friday morning to check her over and give her an injection. And still it rained. But with Ruby settled, a long day was stretching out in front of Phinn. Ty might be home tonight—but how to fill in those yawning hours between now and then? Then she had another idea.

One of the outbuildings had come in for modernisation when Ty had purchased Broadlands, and now served as the estate office. But so far Phinn had not seen the inside of it, and doubted that Ash had spent very much time in there either.

Bearing in mind, if village gossip had been correct, that Ash might have endured some kind of breakdown when working in an office environment, Phinn was wary of suggesting anything that might set him back in any way, but after she had spent some quality time with Ruby, Phinn went looking for him. She found him in the drawing room, staring out of the window at the rain.

'It's a lovely spot here,' she commented when, having heard her come in, Ash looked round.

'It is,' he agreed.

'I've just walked past the estate office. It struck me—I've never seen the inside of it.'

'I wish I didn't have to,' Ash muttered, explaining, 'I've been very neglectful. The paperwork is piling up in there.'

'Hmm...' Phinn murmured, and then offered lightly, 'Do you know, Ash? Today just might be your lucky day.' And, at his querying look, 'It just so happens that I'm a qualified secretary, with a certificate that says I'm good in office administration.'

Ash looked at her in surprise. 'No?'

'Yes,' she replied. And then offered, 'I bet together we could lick your paperwork into shape in no time.'

'You're on!' He grabbed at the offer.

Before she could think further they were out of the house, had the office door unlocked and the lights switched on against the dull day. In no time they were hard at it, tackling the paperwork.

They worked steadily through the rest of the morning, with Phinn keeping an eye on Ash in case the work they were doing was having any ill effect. It wasn't. In fact the more of the backlog they cleared, the brighter Ash seemed to become.

'Oh, Ty's already dealt with that,' he said at one point, having unearthed a letter from Noel Jarvis, enquiring about the possibility of Noel and his son purchasing Yew Tree Farm. 'It seems he phoned Ty in London when his letter here went unanswered.'

'That's probably why we went there last Saturday,' Phinn commented.

'It was,' Ash confirmed. 'Apparently the previous owner of Broadlands always refused to split up the estate. But with Ty saying I can have Honeysuckle Farm if I want it, he's quite happy to sell Yew Tree to the Jarvises. Ty said they have kept it in splendid shape all these years, and ought to have it—' He broke off. 'Oh, Phinn, I'm sorry. I wasn't meaning that Honeysuckle...'

'Don't apologise, Ash,' Phinn said quickly, feeling that she had grown up quite a lot recently. As short a while ago as last week she would have been upset to hear anyone compare Honeysuckle with Yew Tree unfavourably. But last Saturday, when she had felt so awful about the very same thing, Ty had made her feel better.

True, Honeysuckle was a mess. But she could have done little about that—not if she hadn't wanted to make her father's life less fun than it had been. Ty—darling Ty—had put that into perspective for her.

Oh, she did so hope he would come home tonight. It had been an unbearably long week without him. She didn't know if she would be able to take it if he did not come back tonight. She just could not face thinking of the emptiness if he did not come home the entire weekend either!

After a break, while she went and spent some time with Ruby, Phinn returned to the office feeling quite pleased with how much she and Ash had cleared between them. Only some pieces of filing and a few letters to type now, and the office would be more or less as up to date as it was ever going to be.

Phinn was in actual fact tearing away, typing the last of the letters, when—Ash having wandered off to 'get some oxygen to my brain'—the door opened. Her eyes on the page to the left of her, while her fingers raced over the keyboard, she assumed it was Ash returning.

She finished the letter and, as Ash had not made any kind of comment, looked up—and held in a gasp of breath. It was not Ash who had come in but Ty!

Warmth and joy filled her heart. She could not think of a thing to say, and just hoped she had not gone red.

Grey eyes held blue eyes, and then Ty was shaking his head slowly. 'Phinnie Hawkins,' he murmured, 'you never cease to amaze me.'

'Good,' she said impishly, but for no reason felt a touch embarrassed suddenly. 'I used to work as a secretary.'

Again he shook his head slightly. 'You worked as well as kept house?'

Like millions of other women, she didn't doubt. 'You thought all my day consisted of was a little light dusting?' she derided.

'The inside of that farmhouse was shining when I went there,' Ty documented. He paused, and then added, 'But, in addition to keeping the place immaculate, it was *you* who earned to put food on the table.'

Instantly her derision fell from her. She wasn't having that. 'Actually, my father was very clever. He could make, mend, repair and sell things. He was a good provider!' she said stoutly. She wished she hadn't mentioned that her father had sold things as soon as she'd said it. Ty already knew where one of their antiques had gone.

But, as if not wanting to fall out with her, Ty replied seriously, 'You don't have to defend him to me, Phinn. How could he be anything *but* a fine man to have produced such a lovely daughter?'

Phinn looked at him wide-eyed. Oh, my—did he know how to make a girl feel all flustered inside! And yet he had sounded as if he meant it—that 'lovely daughter' bit. 'Okay, so now that we all know you graduated from charm school with honours, what can we do for you?'

'I saw the light on. I thought it was Ash in here,' Ty remarked, and then asked, 'How's he been this week?'

'He's all right,' Phinn assured him. 'He's occasionally a bit down, but generally I think he's picked up quite a bit. Anyhow, I've been watching him today, and he seems fine with the office work.'

'You've been in here most of the day?'

'A lot of it. We've cleared most of the backlog—' Phinn broke off as just at that moment Ash came back.

'What do you think of my new PA?' he asked Ty. And, not waiting for him to answer, 'She's great,' he complimented her. With a smile to her, he looked at his brother to tell him cheerfully, 'In fact, were she not spoken for, I would seriously ask her to consider *me*!'

Phinn smiled happily. She knew that Ash was only teasing, but it was good to see him so uplifted. But when, smiling still, she glanced at Ty, she caught a glimpse of something in his expression that suggested he was not best pleased with his brother's comment.

A second later, however, and she knew that she was mistaken. Because Ty was telling his brother good-humouredly, 'Keep your hands off, Ash,' and then seemed about to depart.

Just to show how little she cared where he went, she said, 'This is the last letter, Ash.' Pretending to be more interested in the job in hand than in either of the Allardyce brothers. 'If you'd like to sign them, I'll take a walk down to the postbox.'

Getting ready to go down to dinner that night, Phinn was again beset by an urge to wear a dress. Crackers—absolutely! She'd lived in trousers for so long now—apart from that one very memorable occasion down at the pool—that she was bound to evoke some sort of comment if she went down wearing something Ash would call 'girly'.

As usual both Ty and Ash were down before her, and, taking her place at the dining table, Phinn felt a flicker of anxiety. She wanted to have a word with Ty later, but was unsure how he would react.

'Did Phinn tell you she frogmarched me down to the pub for a pint yesterday lunchtime?' Ash asked Ty.

Ty turned to her, his grey eyes taking in her wide blue eyes and superb complexion. 'Nothing Phinn does surprises me any more,' he answered lightly. But, with his glance still on her, he asked, 'Are you leading my brother into bad ways?' his mouth curving upward good-humouredly.

'It's my opinion that Ash is perfectly capable of getting into mischief without my help,' she replied, and loved Ty so when he smiled at her. She looked away, got herself under control, and then asked, 'How was your trip?'

The meal passed with Ash asking questions about business and Ty saying that they didn't want to bore Phinn to death—when in truth she wanted to know everything about him. When pressed, he gave a light account of what he had been doing that week.

Phinn started to feel nervous when the meal came to an end and the three of them ambled from the dining room. She felt comfortable enough now not to have to pay a courtesy ten-minute visit to the drawing room with them before she went to see Ruby.

As the two men turned towards the drawing room, and she made to go the other way, she called out, 'Ty!' He halted, and while Ash halted too at first, he must have realised that this was a private moment, because with a hint of a smile on his face he carried on walking.

'Phinn?' Ty encouraged, his eyes on her suddenly anxious face.

'The thing is. Well, I need to see to Ruby now. But—er—can I have a word with you later?'

Ty's expression became grim on the instant. 'If you're thinking of leaving, forget it!' he rapped sharply.

And that rattled her. She was uptight enough without that. 'Forget what I said about charm school!' she erupted, and stormed angrily away from him.

His voice followed her. 'I'll be in my study.'

'Huh!' she snorted in disgust.

As usual, being with Ruby for any length of time calmed her. And really, now that she was calm enough to think about it, Ty sounding so well and truly against her leaving Broadlands was rather flattering.

'So we'll stay, Rubes, my darling,' she told the old mare. 'Not that we've anywhere else to go. I know you like it here—

and between you and me, but don't tell him, it would break my heart to leave.'

All of which put Phinn in a mellow frame of mind when she was ready to go back to the house. Nipping into the downstairs cloakroom to wash her hands, brush any stray bits of straw from her and push tendrils of strawberry-blonde hair from her forehead, Phinn rehearsed what she was going to ask. She didn't know why she felt so nervous. There was no way Ty could refuse.

She left the cloakroom hoping that Ty, aware by now of the length of time she spent with Ruby each evening, would be in his study as he'd said, and that she would not have to go looking for him.

As she went along the hall, she saw that the study door, which was usually closed, now stood open. *Oh, Ty!* She saw it as a sign of welcome, and again felt all squishy inside about him at his thoughtfulness.

Reaching the door, she tapped lightly on it, and her heart did a now familiar flutter as Ty came to the door and invited her in.

'Take a seat,' he offered, indicating a dark brown leather button-back chair and closing the door.

'It won't take that long,' she replied, as he turned to his computer and closed down the work he had been doing.

'You've changed your mind about leaving?' he questioned sternly.

'That was in your head—never in mine!' she replied, wishing she felt better.

'You're certainly looking guilty about something,' he answered shortly.

'No, I'm not!' she exclaimed. Needing some breathing space suddenly, she decided to take the seat he had offered a few seconds ago.

'Has the vet been here?' Ty demanded, taking the office chair and turning it to face her. When Phinn went red—purely because this interview was about money and the vet's bill she couldn't pay, he accused, 'What have you been up to?'—and she could have hit him!

'I haven't been up to anything! And of *course* the vet's been here! Ruby hasn't been well! And if I'm flushed it's not because I'm guilty of anything, but because I'm embarrassed! Honestly!' she fumed.

'Embarrassed? You?'

'Oh, shut up and listen,' she flared, doubting that any of his other employees had ever told him to shut up. But Ty did just that, for he said not another word, and she began floundering to find the right way to say what she had to. Then she realised that after the way this interview had started it just could not get any worse, and so she plunged. 'Is it all right with you if I take a part-time job?'

'You've got a job!' Ty shot back at her forthrightly, before she could blink.

'I know that!' she erupted. 'But this would only be part-time—in the evenings.'

'With the vet?' he charged, before she could draw another breath.

'*No!*' she protested, exasperated. He seemed to have the vet on the brain! 'I just thought that—well, Ruby will be all right on her own for a few hours, and Ash is looking so much better now... His appetite's picked up and he's generally not so—er—bruised as he was, say a month ago. And what with you coming home some evenings to keep him com—'

'If it's not Peverill, who else have you been in contact with?' Ty cut in.

She didn't want to tell him! All this in answer to what to her mind had been a perfectly simple question! Stubbornly she refused to answer. But Ty, at his most unfriendly, was waiting—and not yielding an inch.

'Oh—if you must know—' she exploded, nettled. 'Er...'

Oh, damn the man! 'As Ash mentioned, we went down to the pub yesterday,' she said shortly.

Ty's expression did not lighten any. 'I'm all ears,' he invited.

She sent him a cross look, but had to go on. 'Well, the thing is, I was talking to Bob Quigley…'

'Bob Quigley? Another of your chums?'

'He's the landlord of the Cat and Drum,' she supplied impatiently. Now that she had got started, she wanted it all said and done quickly. Heavens above, it was only a tiddly request, after all!

'So you were talking to Bob Quigley down at the pub…?'

Phinn was about to mention how Ash had seemed to be getting on very well with the new owner of the riding school and stables, but she checked and decided not to—all the quicker to get her request over and done with. 'Well, the upshot of it is, that—well…' She was as impatient with herself as Ty obviously was. 'He—the landlord Bob—offered me a job.'

Ty looked at her with raised brows. 'Behind the bar?' He seemed more amused than anything.

'Yes,' she muttered.

Ty took that on board. 'Know anything about being a pub barmaid?' he enquired coolly, his amused look fading.

'Not the first thing,' she admitted. 'But when I asked Bob if he was fully staffed, he said he would give me a job any time.'

'I'll bet he did!' Ty barked bluntly.

'I wish you'd stop blowing hot and cold!'

'How do you expect me to react? Presumably it's not the company you're after, so what it boils down to is that I'm not paying you enough!'

Feeling contrite suddenly, she said, 'It's not that…' She was embarrassed again, and looked away from him. 'The thing is…'

She glanced back to Ty, and was totally undone when, as if seeing her embarrassment, he changed tack and asked gently, 'What, Phinn? Tell me.'

Phinn took a couple of shaky breaths. 'Well, the thing is, I'm starting to owe the vet big-time. And he's okay about that,' she added quickly. 'He knows that I'll pay him as soon as I can. But…'

'But?' Ty encouraged when she ran out of steam.

'Well, I've owed Kit before. And I didn't mind owing him before. But—well, now that he's asked me out, it—er—makes my debt to him sort of personal, and—well, I'd rather work a couple of hours each evening down at the Cat than leave my account unpaid.'

Ty leaned back in his chair, his expression softening. 'Oh, Phinn Hawkins, what am I going to do with you?' he asked. And then, not really wanting an answer, 'You'd desert us in the evenings, all because Peverill has taken a shine to you?'

She guessed Ty was making light of it because he could see how uncomfortable she was feeling. 'That's about it,' she mumbled. 'Kit's told me there's no hurry, that he knows I'll pay him when I can. But I feel kind of—awkward about it, and…'

'Oh, we can't have that,' Ty said, shaking his head, but finding a smile for her. 'Quite obviously I shall give you a raise.'

'No!' she protested, feeling hot all over. 'I consider I'm overpaid by you as it is.'

'And *I* consider, dear Phinn,' Ty said to make her bones melt, 'that Ash and I would be totally lost without you.'

'Rubbish!'

'Not so. You've no idea how just by being here you brighten the atmosphere. You're so good with Ash—sensing his mood…'

'Tosh!'

'Not to mention that the office has never been straighter than it is today,' he went on, as if she hadn't spoken. 'And, given that I didn't take you on to do secretarial work, that makes me in *your* debt.'

'No!' she denied woodenly.

'You deserve a bonus at least.'

'No!' she maintained.

'Look here, Phinnie.' Ty changed tack again. 'See it from my point of view. You must know that I truly cannot have my girlfriend out working when I come home especially to see her.'

How that made her heart pump overtime! He had so truly sounded as if he really meant it. Thank goodness for common sense. But taking anything personal out of the equation, she could see that Ash might think it a touch peculiar if when Ty came home, *she* went out.

'I…' she said helplessly, and started to feel more anxious than ever.

'Don't worry at it, Phinn,' he instructed. 'I can see exactly why you don't want to owe Peverill—and I think you're quite right. But from my point of view you're doing more than enough here without taking on extra work. So I'll ring the vet and tell him to send Ruby's accounts to me.'

'What for?' she asked, feeling more than a shade bewildered.

'I'll settle them.'

'No, you won't!' she bristled hotly.

'Yes, I will,' he replied firmly—no argument. And, to show that the interview was over, he turned from her and reactivated his computer.

Phinn stared at him. He was not looking at her, and she guessed that since he had been abroad and out of his office all week he wanted her to go so that he could catch up on the week's business events.

With the utmost reluctance, feeling that she could argue with him until she was blue in the face and it would do no good, Phinn, with a heavy sigh but not another word, left his study.

She was on her way upstairs when the unpalatable truth hit her. Ty had appreciated her reason for not wanting to owe the vet because, as he had said, the vet had taken a shine to her. But by that same token Ty had just as good as told her that it was all right for her to owe the vet's bill to Tyrell Allardyce because—quite clearly—he, Ty, had *not* taken a shine to her.

She went to bed mourning that he had not—nor ever would. And spent a sleepless night aware that she was far too unsophisticated to appeal to the sophisticated tastes of Ty Allardyce.

CHAPTER SEVEN

THE weather improved over the weekend and, having been in touch with Bob Quigley to thank him but to tell him she would not be needing a job after all, Phinn was sitting on the paddock rail on Sunday morning watching Ruby. Joy filled Phinn's heart at how well her mare was doing. Then she heard male voices as Ty and Ash came from the house.

A short while later, however, and Ty had left his brother and had come looking for her. He reached her, but for a moment or two said nothing—just observed her in her jeans and tee shirt, with her hair bunched back from her face in a rubber band.

This man she loved so much had the most uncanny knack of making her feel shy! She flicked her glance from him, paying particular attention to climbing down from the fence.

'What have I done wrong now?' she asked, once she was standing beside him.

'Who said you'd done anything wrong?' Ty countered lightly.

'Well, you haven't come over just for a bit of a chat,' she replied, feeling that there must be a reason for Ty coming to seek her out.

He shrugged. 'Could be I thought that—purely to give some authenticity to our relationship—perhaps I should take you out to dinner one evening.'

Her heart spurted again; there was nothing she would like better. But their 'date' wouldn't be for her benefit, but for Ash's. So she stayed outwardly cool to reply, 'We haven't got a relationship.'

'Stop being difficult!' Ty admonished. 'You know how sensitive Ash is. He'll start to wonder soon why you and I—'

'There is no you and I. And anyway, Mrs Starkey is the best cook in these parts. I'd sooner eat her dinners than anyone else's.'

'Difficult, did I say!' Ty grunted. 'Does any man *ever* get to date you?'

'The vet nearly did—once,' she retorted. And oddly, at that shared memory, they both seemed to find it funny—and both grinned.

'Oh, Miss Hawkins,' Ty murmured—which meant nothing, but she thought that perhaps he did quite like her. Then he sobered, and said, 'Actually, Phinn, Ash and I are on our way up to Honeysuckle Farm. Would it be too painful for you to join us?'

After seeing the way Yew Tree Farm had been run last Saturday—the way a farm should be run—Phinn rather thought that to see dilapidated Honeysuckle again would be extremely painful.

'I'd rather not,' she replied quietly, realising that Ash was not the only Allardyce who was sensitive. Ty was sensitive too—in this case to her feelings.

As was proved when he accepted without fuss that she would not visit the farm with them. 'There's every chance that Ash will take over the farm,' he commented.

'I'm sure he'll make a very good job of it,' she replied.

'You don't mind?'

'I'd rather Ash was there than anyone else,' she answered. Ty just stood and looked at her for long, long moments. 'What?' she asked, wondering if she had a smut on her nose.

'D'you know, Phinn Hawkins, you're beautiful inside as well as out?'

Oh, Ty! She wasn't sure that she wasn't going to buckle at the knees, so she turned from him and propped her arms on the fence, looking to where Ruby was happily looking back at her.

'I'm still not going out with you!' she threw over her shoulder—and had to hang firmly on to the rail when Ty did no more than move her bunched hair to one side and planted a warm kiss to the back of her neck—and then departed.

The hours dragged by while Ty was away with Ash, but positively galloped when they came back. And again that Sunday Ty decided to leave it until Monday morning before, extremely early, he left Bishops Thornby for London.

Phinn ached with all she had for him to come back on Monday evening, but it was Wednesday before she saw him again. Ash had gone on his own to spend some more time up at Honeysuckle, and she and Ruby had spent a superb day, with Ruby so much better and the weather perfect.

In fact it was late afternoon when, leaving Ruby in the paddock, Phinn decided to check in the office to see if anything there needed to be attended to. She had her back to the main house and was walking towards the office when she first heard a footfall and then—incredibly—someone behind her calling her name. But not the name she was used to!

'Delphinnium!' The call was soft, the voice male.

She froze. On the instant stood rooted. Then, shocked, she spun swiftly around. There stood Ty, with a grin cracking his face from ear to ear. 'How did you know?' she gasped in amazement. Where had he sprung from? She hadn't heard him arrive!

Ty, enjoying her utter stupefaction, continued to grin. 'I was driving near the church when I saw the vicar,' he answered. 'Very obligingly, he let me look at the baptismal register.'

Starting to recover, she came out fighting. 'If you breathe a word to anyone…' she threatened.

'What's it worth to stay quiet?' Ty asked, not a bit abashed.

But, interested, he enquired, 'Where did you get a name like that anyhow?'

'Blame my father,' she sighed. 'I was supposed to be Elizabeth Maud, only he disobeyed his instructions when he went to register my birth—and thereby guaranteed that his only daughter would remain a spinster throughout the whole of her life.'

'How so?' Ty enquired, looking intrigued.

'With a name like mine, there is absolutely no way,' Phinn began to explain, 'that I'm going to stand up in a white frock in front of any vicar and have my intended roll in the aisle laughing to hear me declare that "I, Delphinnium Hawkins, take you, Joe Bloggs…"'

Ty looked amused, seemed happy to be home, and that gave her joy. 'Your name will be our secret,' he said conspiratorially. And then, while Phinn had drifted off on another front to wonder at the goings-on in this man's clever brain that, when he must have other much more high-powered matters going on in his head, he had paused to check out her name, he was asking, 'Talking of frocks—not necessarily a white one—have you got one?'

'You want to borrow it?' she asked, covering the fact that she was feeling a touch awkward. Was what he was actually saying that he was fed up with seeing her so continually in trousers?

His lips twitched at her retort, but he replied seriously enough. 'Apart from the fact that it's more than high time those fabulous legs had an airing, I've some people coming to dinner on Saturday—a couple of them will be staying overnight.'

'I can have my dinner with Mrs Starkey if—' she began, and saw a sharp look of hostility enter his expression.

'What the blazes are you talking about?' he cut in shortly.

'You won't want me around if you're entertaining,' Phinn tried to explain.

'Give me strength!' Ty muttered. 'If you haven't got it yet, *you, Delphinnium* Hawkins, are part of my family now!' he informed her angrily.

'Not the hired help?' Being short-tempered wasn't his prerogative. 'And don't call me Delphinnium!'

'You're asking for trouble!'

'Trouble is my middle name—and nobody asked you to adopt me!'

Ty gave an exasperated sigh. 'Sometimes I don't know whether I should wallop your backside or kiss you until you beg for mercy!' he snarled.

And, having made him so angry, when he had previously looked so happy, Phinn was immediately contrite. 'Don't be cross with me, Ty,' she requested nicely. 'I'm sorry,' she apologised, and, because he did not look ready to easily forgive her, she went closer and stretched up—and kissed him.

She felt his arms come about her. But he held her only loosely, but his anger was nullified. 'Now who's been to charm school?' he asked.

And she grinned. 'For you, I'll come to your table on Saturday. And for you—I'll wear a dress.'

His grey eyes stared down into her blue ones. 'You'd better clear off before I start some kissing of my own,' he growled. But he let her go, and Phinn, her heart drumming, cleared off quickly to the paddock gate.

Ty came home again on Thursday evening, and again on Friday, and by Saturday Phinn knew the names of the two people who would be staying with them overnight. They were brother and sister, Will and Cheryl Wyatt. Cheryl had apparently just sold her apartment and was between accommodation. She was staying with her brother until she found the right property to purchase.

Ruby was off-colour again on Saturday, so Phinn was out of the house with her when the brother and sister arrived, and missed seeing them.

Having gone to her room to clean up, Phinn decided she was
in no hurry to go down again—which gave her plenty of time
to stand under the shower. She shampooed her hair too, and later,
robe-clad and with a towel around her hair, she surveyed her
wardrobe. Her dresses were not too plentiful, and were mainly
Christmas or birthday presents from her mother. But, again
thanks to her mother, what dresses she had were of good quality.

Having surveyed them for long enough, the one that stood
out from all the others was a plain heavy silk classic dress in
a deep shade of red. She did not own any inexpensive fun jewellery, but felt the low neckline called for something. The
dress definitely called for her hair to be other than pulled
back in a band or plaited into a braid. And suddenly Phinn
started to feel nervous. Which was odd, because she had never
felt nervous about meeting new people before!

All the other people expected at dinner, as well as being
his friends, were people Ty did business with, and nerves
were still attacking as the time neared when she knew she must
go downstairs. Standing before the full-length mirror, she
surveyed the finished product. Good heavens—was that her?

She felt like herself, but gone was the lean and lanky, per-
petually trouser-clad female she was used to. In her place was
a tall, slender woman who curved in all the right places.

Her dress was shorter than she remembered—just above
the knee. It seemed strange, ages since she had even last seen
her knees. Was the neckline too low? Not by today's stan-
dards, she knew, but she wasn't used to revealing a bit of
cleavage. Perhaps Grandmother Hawkins' pearls—rescued
by her mother before her father could sell them—would bring
the eye away from her bosom?

Phinn had used only a discreet amount of make-up, but
somehow her wide eyes seemed to be much wider. Because
there was no way the watch Ty had loaned her went with her
outfit, the pearls were her only jewellery.

Her eyes travelled up to her hair, now confined by pins into an elegant twist on the top of her head.

All in all, she did not think she had dressed 'over the top'. She guessed that Ty's friends would be on the sophisticated side, and did not want to let him down. He had more or less asked her to wear a dress, hadn't he? Or—a dreadful thought struck her—had he? Had he just been teasing? They had been talking about 'a frock', hadn't they, when he had asked her if she possessed one?

Had he been joking? He hadn't actually *asked* her to wear a dress, she recalled. Would he be amazed to see her in anything but trousers?

Phinn was just about to make a rapid change into her more usual dinnertime garb when all at once she heard someone tap on her door.

For all of five seconds she was in a fluster. She had no clue who was on the other side of the door, but, glancing at the watch on her bedside table, Phinn saw that it was not yet seven.

She went to the door and opened it the merest trifle. She looked out. Ty stood there. Ty, magnificent in dinner jacket and bow tie. She opened the door wider, feeling better suddenly, with no need to hide what she was wearing. She was glad that Ty had hinted that she might feel more comfortable in a dress. By the look of it, even though it was with friends, tonight's dinner was a semi-formal affair—she would have felt very under-dressed had she stuck to her usual trousers and top.

'Oh, my…!' Ty breathed, his eyes travelling over her as she stood framed in the doorway. 'You look sensational!'

The compliment pleased her, warmed her. 'You're not looking so bad yourself,' she responded, and laughed. She was wearing higher heels than normal, but he still stood above her.

'I feel I should lock you away in a glass case somewhere,' he answered, and—*ooh*, she loved him so.

'That good, eh?' she queried impishly. And in that moment,

for her, there did not seem to be any other people in the world except the two of them.

'Stunning,' he replied. 'I'd like to—' Just then the sound of someone at the door came, and Ty broke off. 'Saved by the bell,' he said humorously. 'Ash will see to it. Actually, Phinn, I notice you aren't wearing a watch. If you feel lost without one, I thought you might agree to borrow this.' And, putting his hand into his dinner jacket pocket, he withdrew the watch he had tried to give her before.

'You were supposed to have taken that back to the jewellers!' she exclaimed.

'I tried. They wouldn't have it,' he lied—quite blatantly.

'Tyrell Allardyce!' she admonished.

'Yes, sweet Delphinnium?' he replied—and she just had to laugh.

She took the watch from him. 'I'll return it to you tomorrow,' she said.

'Agreed,' he answered, without argument.

And she smiled. 'If I wasn't wearing lipstick, I'd kiss you,' she commented.

'Don't let that stop you,' he encouraged.

'I hear voices. I believe your guests are waiting for you.'

'Damn,' he said—and so started the most wonderful evening of her life.

Ty's friends-cum-business associates ranged in age from late twenties to late forties. There were seven of them in all, and Phinn tried to remember their names as the introductions were made—with not one of them questioning who she was and why she was there.

There were ten seated at the large round dinner table. Phinn was seated opposite Ty, which suited her well, because it gave her the opportunity of glancing at him every so often. Funnily enough, it seemed to her that every time she looked across to him that Ty was looking back at her.

She realised then that her imagination must be working overtime, so concentrated on chatting to Will Wyatt, who was around the same age as Ty, and who was seated on her right. She chatted equally to the man on her left, an older man named Kenneth.

In talking to the two men, and feeling quite at ease with them, Phinn discovered that she had more general knowledge than she had realised. She knew that she had her father to thank for that because, aside from taking her to museums and art galleries, it had been her father who had encouraged her to ask questions and form her own opinions. It had been her father with whom she had discussed the merits and de-merits of painters and writers. And it was all there in her head—just waiting to be tapped.

'What do you think of Leonardo?' Kenneth asked at one point.

'A true genius,' Phinn answered, always having much admired Leonardo da Vinci—and then she and Kenneth were in deep discussion for the next ten minutes, until Will Wyatt accused Kenneth of monopolising her.

'I have the advantage of being married—to my good lady here,' Kenneth replied, looking to his wife, who was deep in conversation with the man to the left of her. 'Therefore Phinn is quite safe with me. You, on the other hand, young Will…'

In no time the three of them were laughing. It was then that Phinn happened to glance across to Ty. He was not laughing. He wasn't scowling either. He was just—looking. Feeling all mixed-up inside, Phinn stayed looking at him, her brain seeming to have seized up. Then Cheryl Wyatt, seated to the left of Ty, placed a possessive hand on his arm to draw his attention—and all of a sudden, as Ty glanced to Cheryl and smiled, Phinn was visited by another emotion. An emotion that had visited her briefly once before and was one she did not like. Jealousy.

It was the only small blip of the evening.

Wendy and Valerie, Mrs Starkey's usual helpers in the house, had been roped in to help serve the meal. But when everyone adjourned to the drawing room afterwards, Phinn took off kitchenwards.

She was in the throes of telling Mrs Starkey how well everything had gone when Ty appeared, on the very same errand.

'Thank you, Mrs Starkey. Everything was perfect,' he said, and Mrs Starkey beamed with pride. Phinn guessed she and her staff would be well rewarded for their efforts, and moved towards the kitchen door.

She went out into the hall feeling a touch awkward suddenly. A moment later Ty was joining her, and they were strolling back along the hall.

'I don't want you to think—' she began in a rush, but was stopped when Ty placed a hand on her arm and halted her. 'I—er…' She faltered. He waited, saying nothing, just standing there looking down at her as if he liked looking at her. 'I know—er—I mean I know I'm not the hostess here…'

'A very lovely hostess you would make,' he put in lightly.

Which did little to ease her feeling of awkwardness. 'I wanted to thank Mrs Starkey—' She broke off. 'I didn't know if…'

'If I would think to do so?' Ty looked kindly down at her. 'Who else would I expect to do the honours for me, little Phinn, but an adopted member of my family?'

'Oh, Ty,' she said softly, and didn't know just then quite how she felt.

If Ty included her as his family because he felt under some kind of obligation, because through her he still had a brother, then she did not want to be part of his family. If, on the other hand, he regarded her as family because he enjoyed having her under his roof—albeit temporarily—then there was nothing she would like better than to be considered part of his family. But she could never explain that to him—not without the risk of showing him how very much she loved him.

She opted to change tack. 'By the way, I meant to thank *you*. Kit Peverill says you rang him and asked him to forward all the accounts for Ruby's care to you.'

'You've seen Peverill?' Ty asked sharply. 'Has he been here?'

Phinn looked at him, exasperated. 'You're never the same two minutes together!' she erupted. 'Of *course* he's been here. I've an elderly horse. I want a vet who's local—a vet who knows me, who knows Ruby, who I can trust to drop everything but emergencies when I call!' She gave a heated sigh, and, having got that off her chest, an impish look came into her eyes. 'Hmm…Kit said, incidentally, that he hadn't known that *you* were the man I had just started seeing until your call about the account. He rather put two and two together and assumed… Anyhow, at just that point his phone rang with an emergency, and he'd gone before I could tell him differently. Er…'

'There's more?'

'It's just that this is a small village, and while I'm sure Kit won't gossip, he'll only have to say some small thing in passing about me having a boyfriend and it will be all over the place before you can blink.'

Phinn half supposed she'd expected Ty to be cross—for all it was more his doing than hers. But he wasn't cross—not at all. He merely replied equably, 'I reckon my shoulders are broad enough to take it.'

'Fine,' Phinn murmured, and moved on. But when they came to the part of the hall where he would turn into the drawing room to join his guests, she halted briefly to ask, 'Would you mind if I went along to see Ruby?'

'You'll be missed,' Ty replied.

Her heart gave a giddy flip at the ridiculous idea that Ty, personally, would miss her. 'There goes that charm again!' she scorned humorously, and headed for the outside door.

She was not the only one outside, Phinn soon discovered, because she was on her way to the stable when Will Wyatt called out, 'Where are you off to?'

She turned, startled. 'What are you doing out here?' she asked lightly.

'When you disappeared I thought I might as well ease my sorrows with a cigar,' Will replied. 'Wherever you were dashing off to, can I come too?' he asked.

Charm, she rather thought, was catching. 'Do you like horses?'

'Love them!' he said promptly, and as promptly stamped out his cigar.

Ruby had picked up again, but Phinn knew from experience that it did not mean that she would stay up. Phinn introduced her to Will Wyatt, who was lovely and gentle with her, and she warmed to him.

They were still with Ruby when her ears twitched, and a few seconds later Ty appeared, with Cheryl Wyatt in tow. 'Ty thought we'd find you here!' Cheryl exclaimed. But, as if she understood that Ruby had health problems, she was gentle with her too, and Phinn found she liked the other woman— if not the possessive way she was hanging on to Ty's arm.

'We'll leave you to say goodnight to Ruby,' Ty commented, edging Cheryl towards the door, and turning as though waiting for Will to join them.

Will didn't look as if he was likely to take the hint, so it was left to Phinn to look at him and say, as though making a general comment, 'I won't be long.'

They were a good group, Ty's friends, and time flew by until all but Will and Cheryl Wyatt made to depart. Apparently the departing guests all had properties out of London, either in Gloucestershire or one of the neighbouring counties.

Shortly after they had gone, Phinn took a glance to the lovely watch she had on and was amazed to see that it had gone midnight! 'If no one minds, I think I'll go up,' she said, to no one in particular.

'Do you have to?' Will asked.

'I shall be up early in the morning,' she replied, because he was so nice.

'Then so shall I,' he answered.

'Er—good,' she said politely. She would be getting up early to go and check on Ruby; she had no idea what Will intended to do.

By morning she discovered that he did, as he had said, love horses. He came into the stable at six o'clock to see Ruby anyhow. That morning Phinn was dressed in her usual jeans and a tee shirt, with her hair pulled back in a rubber band. It did not seem to put him off.

'Ever get up to London?' he enquired as she got busy with a pitchfork.

'Not usually,' she replied.

'If you fancy it, I'd like to take you to a show. You needn't worry about getting back. You could stay the night.'

Phinn gave him a startled look.

'Cheryl will be there too!' he hurriedly assured her, correctly interpreting Phinn's look. 'I didn't mean…'

Phinn forgave him. She was in the middle of thanking him for his invitation, but refusing, when Ty came in and joined them.

'Couldn't sleep?' he asked his friend Will.

'The bed was bliss,' Will replied. 'I was just asking Phinn to come to a show with me—Phinn could stay overnight with Cheryl and me, and…'

'Phinn wouldn't want to leave Ruby overnight.' Ty refused for her.

'You or Ash could look after her for one night, surely?' Will turned to Ty to protest.

Phinn shook her head. 'Thank you all the same, Will, but no way.'

'Mrs Starkey is making an early breakfast,' Ty cut in, and as Phinn got on with her chores, Will, so not to offend his host or his host's cook, went with him.

Will did not ask her out again, but came to find her when they all decided to go for a long walk—exercise needed after the previous evening's dinner and this morning's full breakfast. 'Do come with us,' he urged. 'Ash tells me there's not a thing about this area that you don't know.'

Perhaps because she fancied a walk, Phinn went with them—though was not too enamoured that more often than not Cheryl appeared to be walking with Ty, as though his partner.

Brother and sister left shortly after lunch, with Will kissing Phinn's cheek and saying he would be in touch. But as soon as Broadlands returned to normal, Phinn went to chat with Ruby.

Nobody wanted very much in the way of food at dinnertime. And with Ty spending time in his study catching up, and Ash in one of the other rooms watching one of his favourite programmes on television, Phinn went first to see Ruby, and then decided to turn in.

She was in her pyjamas, face scrubbed, body showered, hair brushed out of the band it had been in all day, when she remembered the watch. Ty was staying tonight, but would be leaving very early in the morning for London. She was tempted to take it along to his room, but...

But why not? Ty was not averse to popping into her room when he wanted to leave her salary cheque. And anyway, he was in his study downstairs. It would only take but a moment, and she would by far prefer that the expensive watch was in his possession before he went off tomorrow. He was off on his travels again, so heaven only knew when he would be home again.

Not giving herself time to think further, and just in case anyone was about, Phinn threw on a light robe. She was by then aware of which room was Ty's and, picking up the dainty watch, she quickly left her room. At his door, for form's sake, she tapped lightly on the wood paneling, but not waiting for an answer quickly went straight in.

Only to stop dead in her tracks! The light was on, and Ty was not downstairs in his study as she had been so sure he was. Barefooted, his shirt unbuttoned prior to his taking a shower—or whatever was his normal night-time procedure—there he stood.

'I'm sorry—sorry!' Phinn exclaimed, flustered, realising she must have been in her bathroom cleaning her teeth and so had not heard him passing her door. She held out the watch while at the same time wanting to back to the door. 'I thought you were downstairs. Only I—um—wanted this watch in your safekeeping before you left.'

Ty didn't move, and made no attempt to take the watch from her but, as if women entering his bedroom was an everyday event—and she did not want to think about *that*—he invited, 'Come in and talk to me,' doing up a couple of shirt buttons as he spoke. 'I don't bite.' And when she looked at him, a touch startled by his invitation, 'Well, not usually anyway,' he said, the corners of his wonderful mouth picking up.

But Phinn, while she would have liked nothing better than to talk to him, looked down at her thin pyjamas and lightly robed self. 'What do you want to talk about?' she asked. It might be normal for him to chat the night away with women in their night clothes, but it was a first for her.

'Well, you might want to tell me how you enjoyed the weekend, for one thing?' Ty suggested.

'I did,' she replied. Ruby had picked up again, so all was right with her world.

'You liked my friends?'

He asked as if it mattered to him that she should like his friends. That thought warmed her, and Phinn for the moment forgot she was feeling awkward. Since Ty wasn't attempting to take the watch from her, she stepped further into his room and placed it down on top of a mahogany chest of drawers.

'Very much,' she answered. 'Kenneth made me laugh, and I thought his wife, Rosemary, was sweet.'

'You know you were a big hit with them,' he commented, moving casually to close the door.

Phinn looked at him, again startled, as the door closed. 'Er—you're not going to attempt to seduce me, are you?' she asked warily.

Ty burst out laughing, his superb mouth widening. 'What a delight you are!' he remarked, but replied, 'That wasn't my intention, but if you...?' He left the rest of it unsaid, but his mouth was still terrifically curved in a grin. 'I just thought we could have a private moment or two while you let me know what you're going to tell Will Wyatt when he rings.'

'What makes you think he's going to ring?'

'You know he is. He's totally captivated by you.'

She would not have put it as strongly as that. 'He's nice,' she commented.

'You're not going out with him,' Ty stated more than asked.

'As Your Lordship pleases,' she responded, and just had to laugh.

'Are you making fun of me?' Ty asked, coming a dangerous couple of steps nearer.

'Would I dare?' she asked demurely.

'I wouldn't put it past you to dare anything, Phinn Hawkins,' Ty answered. And, when she looked as though she would turn about and go, 'Do you want to go out with him?' he demanded, with no sign of a grin about him now.

It did not take any thinking about. The only man she wanted to go out with was the one standing straight in front of her. 'I'm not going up to London to go out with him, and since I

wouldn't want to leave Ruby for more than a couple of hours,
I can't see any point in him coming down here to take me out.'

'Which doesn't answer my question.'

'I know,' she replied impishly.

'You *do* know you're likely to drive some man insane?'

'You say the sweetest things.'

Ty looked at her mischievous expression, his glance going
down to her uptilted mouth. 'You'd better go!' he said abruptly,
and brushed past her as though to go and open the door.

But he did not make it because, her pride rearing at being
thrown out—dammit, it was *he* who had asked her to stay!—
Phinn at the same time moved smartly to the door. And
somehow they managed to collide slap-bang into each other.

Angrily, Phinn put out her arms to save herself, but
somehow found that she was holding on to Ty. And Ty, in his
efforts for stability, somehow had his hands on her waist. And
then, as they looked into each other's eyes, it was as if neither
could resist the other.

Ty let out a groan, his words seeming to be dragged from
him. 'I want to kiss you.'

Phinn shook her head to say no, but found that the person
in charge of her was saying, quite huskily, 'If memory serves,
you kiss quite nicely, Tyrell Allardyce…' The rest didn't get
said. It was swallowed up as Ty's head came down and his
lips met hers.

It was one very satisfying kiss, but at last he raised his head
from hers. 'You don't kiss too badly yourself,' he commented
softly, looking deeply into her eyes.

'I do my best,' she answered, mock-demurely.

'Want to go for seconds?' he questioned lightly, and, while
she was unsure what Ty meant by that, what she did know was
that to be in his arms was pure and utter bliss and she never
wanted it to stop.

Unsure what to answer, Phinn followed her instincts and

stretched up and kissed him. And that was all the answer he needed because, lightly at first, Ty was returning that kiss, and bliss just did not begin to cover it. Her heart rejoiced to be this close to him, to be held in those firm arms.

Her arms went around him and as he held her so she held him. She could feel his body through her thin clothing and loved the closeness with him. Yet even as Ty ignited a fire in her, she found she wanted to get yet closer.

She felt his hand at the back of her head, his lips leaving hers as he buried his face in her long, luxurious strawberry-blonde hair. And then his lips were finding hers again—and she knew that as she wanted him, so Ty wanted her.

With his arms around her, he pulled her to him. 'Sweet darling,' he murmured, and she was in a mindless world where she *was* his sweet darling.

For how long they stood, delighting in each other's kisses, Phinn had no idea, but only knew that she was with him wherever he led.

A small spasm of nervousness attacked her, nevertheless, when, compliant in his arms, she let Ty move with her to the inviting king-size bed. But, incredibly, he seemed to notice her hesitation, for, with his arms still around her, he paused and looked down into her slightly flushed face.

'Everything right with you?' he asked tenderly—and she was utterly enchanted.

She looked tenderly back and found her husky voice to say, 'Oh, yes,' and to add, 'But I do believe you *are* seducing me.'

Ty smiled into her eyes. 'Believe?' he echoed. 'Don't you know?'

She smiled back. She loved him. What else mattered? She wondered if she should tell him that she had never been this way with a man before, but did not want him to think her a fool, so instead she kissed him. And Ty needed no further encouragement.

Phinn was enraptured when he undid her robe and slid it from her shoulders. And she loved, adored him when, once she was clad only in her pyjama shorts and a thin-strapped pyjama top, his eyes travelled down over her.

Ty took her in his arms once more, and then she realised that they had been merely skating around the preliminaries, because with a gradually increasing passion Ty was teaching her what lovemaking was all about.

She felt his warm hands come beneath her thin top, felt those hands warm on the skin of her spine, and was drowning at his every spine-tingling touch.

When those same hands moved to the front of her and, seeking ever upwards, he at last captured her breasts, her cry of sweet rapture mingled with his groan of wanting.

He kissed her, moulding and caressing her breasts as his kiss deepened. But, as if tormented beyond reason at the sight of her, as if tormented to uncover the splendour in his hold, Ty pulled back. 'I want to see you,' he breathed.

Phinn swallowed hard to hide her shyness. 'I want to see you too,' she murmured huskily, and got her wish when, unhurriedly, Ty removed his shirt.

His chest was magnificent and she stared in wonder before leaning forward and placing a kiss there. And she was delighted when, as she leaned forward, Ty pulled her top over her head. Then, as she stood before him, her top half uncovered, he pulled back to study her. 'Oh, my sweet one,' he said softly, as he surveyed her creamy swelling full breasts with their hardened pink tips. 'You are totally exquisite.' And he took first one hardened pink peak into his mouth, then released it to taste the sweetness of the other.

Phinn swallowed hard when his hands went to the waistband of his trousers, and buried her face in his shoulders. Then she knew more bliss—utter bliss—when they stood thigh to thigh. His hands at her back, he caressed unhurriedly downwards.

His body was a delight to her, 'Oh, Ty,' she cried. 'I want you so much.'

'And I you, sweet darling,' he murmured, and moved with her as though to take her to lie down on the bed with him.

But while Phinn was unaware that she had made any slight movement of hesitation, Ty seemed to sense one. Because he paused, his glance gentle on her. Just that—no movement. Just waiting. If she had any objection to make, now—even at this late stage—was the time to state it.

And, looking at him, Phinn almost told him that she loved him, but somehow felt that that was not what he would want to hear. So instead, foolish or not, she realised that in all fairness she ought to say something.

'Er...' she began hesitantly. 'I'm, er—a bit...'

The words seemed to stick in her throat, but Ty wasn't going anywhere. With his warm hands still holding her, he said gently, 'You want to make love with me, but you're a bit...?' And, as if he simply could not resist her gorgeous breasts, he bent to kiss them.

'Well...' She took a steadying breath as he pulled back to look at her. 'Have you any idea what you're doing to me?' she asked, side-tracked, the feel of his mouth at her breast still with her.

'If it's anything similar to what you're doing to me, I'd say it's pretty dynamic,' he answered, and smiled, and kissed her—but made no move to lie down with her. 'You're a bit—what?' he prompted gently again.

'Well, the thing is—I'm not at all sure how these things go...but I—er...'

'Tell me, sweet love,' he invited, when she got stuck again.

And suddenly she wanted it all said and done quickly. 'The thing is...' she began in a rush, then halted, got her second wind, and rushed on again. 'Well, I feel a bit of a fool because I've no idea whether you need to know to not but...' Oh, heavens, so intimate, half undressed, nearly completely undressed, and still those private words would not come! That was until, totally impatient with herself, she burst out, 'I've no idea if you need to know that I've never—um—been this f-far before.'

On the instant Ty stilled, his expression changing from that of a tender ardent lover to disbelief at what it sounded as if she was saying. Then his look changed to one of utter astonishment as it started to quickly sink in, and from astonishment to a look of being completely shaken.

Ty was stern faced as he gripped hard on to her naked shoulders. 'Just what, exactly,' he urged—a little hoarsely, she thought, 'are you saying?'

'Well, I wasn't sure… That is, I don't know if I'm supposed to say, or if it's all right for you to just—er—find out, but…'

'Oh, my God!' He was incredulous. 'You're a virgin!' He seemed stunned.

'Does it matter?' she asked, feeling more than a touch bewildered—and heard Ty take what she assumed to be a long-drawn steadying breath.

'Right at this moment,' he commented tautly, 'I want you more than you can know.' His glance moved down to her breasts and he gave a groan as he ordered, 'For sanity's sake, cover yourself up!' And when Phinn, more than a little confused at what he was saying, was not quick enough, he swiftly picked up her thin robe from the carpet and as quickly wrapped it around her. Then, running a fevered hand across his forehead, he said, 'I want you, Phinn. Don't mistake that. But I need space to try and think straight.'

Phinn stared at him. She felt even more unsure, which made her feel nervous—and a fool. And a split second later she knew, while the rest of her brain was just so much of a mish-mash, that the moment was lost! Knew with crystal clarity that she was never ever going to know the full joy of sharing her body with Ty, the man she loved.

And in the next split second, while everything in her still cried out for her to be his, her pride began to stir. And as her pride started to surge upwards because Ty needed to *think* whether to reject her *or not*—so her pride took off and rocketed into orbit. *Reject her!* 'Take all the time and space you need,' she exploded furiously—damn it, her voice was still husky. 'I'm leaving.'

'Phinn, don't—' Ty tried to get in.

'I won't!' she hurled at him, and was already on her way. 'Trust me—I won't.'

CHAPTER EIGHT

THE hours until dawn were long and painful. Ty might have said that he wanted her and not to make any mistake about that. But that he'd had to *think* about it showed that he could not have wanted her as much as he had said he did.

Her watch—his watch—showed it was just before four when Phinn heard the faint sound of Ty leaving the house. She wanted to leave too, and never to come back.

She had told him she had wanted him. For heaven's sake, what more proof did he need that she was his for the taking? She had stood—she blushed—semi-naked in front of him. And he—he had rejected her!

In fear and mortification that Ty might have seen that she loved him, that she had given away her feelings for him, Phinn wanted to run and hide. To run and hide and never to have to see him again. But she could not leave—there was Ruby.

Phinn spent many countless, useless minutes in wondering what, if anything, Ty thought about her. But in the end, with more scorched cheeks, she realised that from his point of view making love with her did not have to mean that he cared anything about her at all. Given that once the kissing had started they had soon established there was a certain chemistry between them, from Ty's point of view it did not have to mean a thing.

Nursing sore wounds, Phinn showered and dressed early and went to see Ruby. Phinn had sometimes wondered through Ruby's various bouts of illness if, for Ruby's sake, she was wrong not to have her put down. But as she spoke gently to her that morning, and Ruby nuzzled into her, Phinn knew that she could never do that.

That Monday was a busy day for phone calls. Her mother rang, and Phinn again promised to try to go and see her soon. And Will Wyatt rang, asking her not to forget him and telling her that he was working on a plan to get Ty to invite him for a long weekend soon.

In a weak moment Phinn wondered if Ty would ring. But that was fantasy, for he never did. And why would he, for goodness' sake? He lived in a fast-paced sophisticated environment, where sophisticated women abounded. He hadn't the time nor the inclination—obviously—to bring a 'village local' virgin up to speed.

Realising she was in danger of letting what was now firmly fixed in her head as Ty's rejection of her sour her outlook, Phinn turned her back on the memory of Ty's unbelievable tenderness and his heady passion with her, and concentrated on why she was there.

'Where are you off to, Ash?' she asked him, when she saw him setting off across the fields. He was so much better now than he had been, so much brighter all round, that she had begun to feel that her role in watching him was now more or less redundant. But Ty was paying her to be Ash's companion, and whatever feelings went on in her head about Ty, a job was a job.

'I thought I'd stretch my legs and think about farming matters.'

'Shall I come with you?'

That was Monday.

On Tuesday, with Ruby once more in fine fettle, Phinn again latched on to Ash when he said he was going up to

Honeysuckle Farm with a view to checking out some improvements he wanted to make. By then, with Ty so constantly in her head, her aversion to going to the neglected farm where she had been brought up seemed to be secondary.

Bearing in mind she was being well paid to keep Ash company, when she saw him making for the pick-up on Wednesday, she went over to him. But before she could open her mouth to invite herself to go along too, wherever he was going, Ash beat her to it.

'Phinn—dear Phinn,' he began sensitively, 'as my honorary sister, I love you dearly. But would you mind if just this once I went out on my own?'

Phinn looked at him. He had put on weight, the dark shadows had gone from beneath his eyes, and he was a world away from the wretched, heartsore man she had known a couple of months ago.

She was not in the least offended, and grinned at him as she replied, 'Depends where you're going.'

For a moment or two he looked as though he wasn't going to tell her. But then—just a touch sheepishly, Phinn thought—he answered, 'If you must know, I thought I'd meander over to Geraldine Walton's place and see how she feels about having dinner with me on Saturday night.'

Phinn just beamed at him. 'Oh, Ash. I couldn't be more pleased!' she exclaimed.

'She hasn't said yes yet!'

She would, Phinn knew it. 'Best of luck,' she bade him, and went to chat to Ruby.

By the look of it, her work at Broadlands was done—and that was worrying. Matters financial were crowding in on her, but Phinn could not see how she could continue to take a salary from Ty when she wasn't doing anything.

By afternoon, however, Phinn had something more to worry about. Ruby had stopped eating. Trying not to panic, Phinn rang Kit Peverill, who was out at one of the neighbouring farms but said he would call in on his way back. Which he did.

'Doesn't look too good, Phinn,' he said, after examining Ruby.

Phinn's low spirits dropped to zero. She clenched her jaw as tears threatened. 'Is she in pain?'

'I'll give her an injection to make her comfortable,' he replied. 'It should last her a couple of days, but call me sooner if you need to.'

Phinn thanked him, and as he went down the drive she saw Ash returning in the pick-up. 'How did it go?' she asked Ash, but had no need to. The smile on his face said it all.

'As you yourself have discovered—who could resist the Allardyce charm?' He grinned.

Who, indeed? But she had other matters on her mind just then. 'Was that the vet's Land Rover I passed in the drive?'

'Ruby's not so good.'

Sympathetically, Ash went back with her to see Ruby, who seemed to Phinn to be losing ground by the hour. Phinn had no appetite either, and spent the rest of the day with Ruby, only leaving when Ash came and said that Mrs Starkey was preparing a tray for her.

'I'll come in,' Phinn told him. No way could she eat in front of the sick mare.

Ash, Phinn discovered, had turned into her minder. He took turns with her in staying with Ruby. And, because Ruby had taken to Ash, with his gentle way of talking to her, Phinn left Ruby with him when she needed to shower, or to try to get down the sandwich Mrs Starkey had provided for her.

Phinn called in Kit Peverill again on Thursday—his expression told her what Phinn would not ask.

Phinn stayed with Ruby the whole of Thursday night. Ruby died on Friday morning. Phinn did not know how she would bear it—but Ash was marvellous.

Ash might not have been at his best in an office environment, but when Ruby died he more than showed his worth. As Ruby went down, Ash took charge. And Phinn was never more grateful.

'I'll go and phone the vet and make all the other necessary phone calls while you say goodbye to her, darling,' he said gently. 'Leave everything to me.' With that, he left the stable.

An hour later Phinn left Ruby. She saw Ash without actually seeing him, and, her face drained of colour, went walking.

For how long she walked over land that she had once ridden over with Ruby, she had no idea. She was miles from the house when she came to a spot where she and Ruby had unexpectedly come across a recently fallen tree trunk. She could feel Ruby's joy as they had sailed right over it even now. Ruby was not a jumper, and they had both been exhilarated. Ruby had given her a look that Phinn would have sworn said, *Hey—did you see me do that?*

When Phinn returned to the stable, hours later, the vet had been and gone—and so too was Ruby gone. The stable doors were open, the stable cleaned and hosed down by Ash, and Ash was coming over to her.

'They took her as gently as they could,' he promised. 'I've arranged to collect her ashes—I thought you might want to scatter them over her favourite places.' And, looking into her face, 'You look tired,' he observed. 'Come on, Mrs Starkey's got some of your favourite soup waiting for you.'

More or less on automatic pilot, Phinn went and had some soup, was fussed over by Mrs Starkey, and told to go and rest by Ash. Phinn felt too numbed to argue, and went and lay on her bed.

She thought she might have slept for a while, but she felt lifeless when she awakened. She took a shower and changed into fresh trousers and a shirt. She felt a need to do something, but had no idea what.

Brushing her hair, she pulled it back in a band and went outside. She did not want to go into the stable, but found her feet taking her there. It was where Ash found her some ten minutes later.

Leaving the stable together, they walked out into the late-afternoon sun. 'I don't know of anything that's going to make you feel any better, Phinn, but if you want me to come walking with you, want me to drive you anywhere, or if you'd like me to take you out somewhere for a meal, you've only to say.'

Phinn had held back tears all day, but as she turned to him her bottom lip trembled and she knew that she was close to breaking. 'Oh, Ash,' she mumbled, and liked him so much, felt true affection for him, when, placing a gentle arm around her, he gave her a hug. Needing his strength for just a brief moment, Phinn held on to him.

It *was* only a brief moment, however, because suddenly she became aware that there was a car parked in front of the house—a car she had not heard pull up.

It was Ty's car, and he was standing next to it, looking their way. Ash had not seen him, but Phinn could not miss the fact that Ty was positively glaring at her! Even from that distance there was no chance of missing that he was furious about something. Something so blisteringly anger-making that a moment later, as if he did not trust himself, Ty had swung abruptly to his right and gone striding indoors.

So much for her wondering, as she had so often since last Sunday, how she was ever going to face him again. Forget tenderness, forget gentleness Ty had looked as though he could cheerfully throttle her!

With a shaky sigh, Phinn stepped out of Ash's hold. 'You've been a gem today, Ash,' she said softly. 'I'll never forget it.'

'I'm here for you, love,' he said, but let her go when she pulled out of his hold. 'I'm going to the office. Want to come?'

Phinn shook her head. She felt lost, and didn't know where she wanted to go. But the sanctuary of her room was as good a place as any.

Before she could get there, however, she had to run the gauntlet of one very thunderous-looking Tyrell Allardyce. She had hoped he might be in the drawing room, his own room or his study, and that she might be able to reach her room without seeing him.

So much for hope! Phinn had barely stepped into the hall when Ty, as if waiting for her, appeared from his study. His demeanour had not sweetened any, she noted. As was proved when, looking more hostile than she had ever seen him, 'In my study—*now*!' he snarled.

Go to blazes and take your orders with you, sprang to her mind. But, since he was obviously stewed up about something— forget 'sweet darling'—she'd better go and get it over with.

Phinn walked towards him, past him and into his study. But she had hardly turned before he had slammed the door shut and was demanding explosively, 'Just what the hell sort of game do you think you're playing?'

Phinn sighed. She really did not need this. Yet how dear he was to her. She wanted to hate him. But, furious with her or tender with her, she loved him in all his moods.

'I'm—not with you,' she replied quietly.

'Like hell you're not! How long's it been going on?'

She still wasn't with him. 'How long has what been going on?'

Ty gave her a murderous impatient look. 'Naïve you might be, but you're not *that* naïve,' he roared, and Phinn, having been spent all day, started to get angry.

'Don't throw that back at me!' she erupted, warm colour rushing to her face at his reference to her having disclosed to him, in a very private moment, that she was inexperienced.

'I'll do whatever I like!' Ty fired back. 'You're here to

look after my brother, not to try and send him down the same downward spiralling road your cousin did!'

'That's most unfair!' Phinn charged hotly.

'Is it?' he challenged, with no let up in his fury. 'What's your plan? To trot into his bedroom one night when he's half undressed and have a crack at losing your virginity with him too?'

Crack was the operative word. Without being aware of what she was doing, but incensed and in sudden fury that Ty could so carelessly demean something that had been so very special to her, infuriated beyond bearing that he could say such a thing, Phinn hit him! She had never hit anybody in her life. But all her strength went into that blow.

The sound of her hand across Ty's cheek was still in the air when Phinn came to her senses. She did not know then who was the more appalled—her or Ty. He by what, in his fury, he had just said—she by what, in her fury, she had just done. Either way, it was clear, as he stared dumbfounded at her, that no female had ever hit him before.

Phinn felt absolutely thunderstruck herself as she stared at the red mark she had created on the side of his face. 'Oh, Ty,' she mourned, tears spurting to her eyes, a tender, remorseful hand going up to that red mark. 'I'm so sorry.' Still Ty looked at her, as if speechless. 'I'm—a bit upset,' she understated.

'*You're* upset!' he exclaimed.

'Ruby…' she managed, and knew then that the floodgates she had kept determinedly closed all day were about to break open.

'Ruby?' Ty questioned, his senses alert, his tone softening.

Had he stayed furious with her, nasty with her, Phinn reckoned she might have been able to hang on until she reached her room. But when Ty, who obviously didn't know about Ruby but had sensed all was not well with her, started to show a hint of sympathy, Phinn lost it. She made a dive for the door, but before she could escape Ty had caught a hold of her.

'Ruby?' he repeated.

'Ruby…' The words would not come. Tears were already falling when she at last managed, 'Ruby—she died today.'

'Oh, sweetheart!' In the next instant Ty had taken her in his arms and was holding her close up to him—and Phinn's heart broke.

Sobs racked her as Ty held her close. He held her and stroked her hair, doing his best to comfort her as tears and sobs she could not control shook her. Having held her emotions in check all day, it seemed that now she had given way she was unable to stop.

Ty was still holding her firm when she at last managed to gain some semblance of control. 'I'm—s-sorry,' she apologised, and attempted to pull away from him. His answer was to hold her more tightly to him. 'I'm sorry,' she repeated. 'I—haven't cried all day.'

'I'm sorry too,' he murmured soothingly. 'And I'm glad I was here when you finally let go the grip on your emotions.'

Phinn took a shaky breath that still had a touch of a sob to it. 'Ash has been marvelous,' she felt she should tell him. 'He saw to everything for me.'

'When he's on form he's good in a crisis,' Ty agreed.

'I'm all right now,' Phinn said, trying to shrug out of his comforting hold.

'You're sure?'

She nodded, wanting to stay exactly where she was. 'I look a mess,' she mumbled.

'You look lovely,' he answered, taking out a handkerchief and gently mopping her eyes, now red from weeping.

'You're a shocking liar,' Phinn attempted, and took a small step backwards.

Ty, still holding her, looked down into her unhappy face. And, oddly, it seemed the most natural thing in the world that they should gently kiss. Phinn took another step back and Ty, as if reluctantly, let her go. Phinn left his study to go up to her room.

It was not the end of her tears. Tears came when she least expected them.

Not wanting to break down again, should tears appear unexpectedly at the dinner table, Phinn went to tell Mrs Starkey not to make dinner for her and say that if anyone asked she had gone to bed.

'Can I make you an omelette, or something light like that, Phinn?' Mrs Starkey asked.

But Phinn shook her head. 'That's very kind of you, Mrs Starkey, but I'm not hungry. I'll just go and catch up on some sleep.'

In actual fact Phinn slept better than she had anticipated. Though she was awake for a long while, and heard first Ash come to bed and then, later, Ty. She didn't know how she knew the difference in the two footfalls, she just did.

She tensed when Ty seemed to halt outside her bedroom door, but she knew that he would not come in. After last Sunday bedrooms were sacrosanct. That was to say she knew she would never again trespass into his bedroom. By the same token—remembering that chemistry between them—Ty was giving *her* bedroom a wide berth.

Having awakened early, at her usual time, Phinn felt tears again spring to her eyes when, throwing back the covers, she realised that there was nothing—no darling Ruby—to dash out of bed for.

Phinn dried her eyes and pulled the covers back over her, and thought back to yesterday. Not Ruby dying—that would live with her for ever. And, while she would always remember her gentle, timid Ruby, Phinn did not want to dwell on her dying. Instead she thought of happier times. Times when she and Ruby had galloped all over Broadlands, the wind in her hair, Ruby as delighted as Phinn.

Fleabitten old nag indeed! But now Phinn was able to smile at the memory. Ty had been pretty wonderful in finding a stable to make Ruby's last days comfortable.

He had been pretty wonderful to her too, when he had come home yesterday, Phinn considered, remembering how he had cradled her to him as she had wept all over him. He had mopped her up and…

And she had hit him, Phinn recalled. Not a tap, but a full-on whack! Oh, how could she? But she wasn't going to think about unpleasant things. She had been down in the pits yesterday and, while she knew she would not get over Ruby in a hurry, Phinn also knew, remembering the dark pit she had descended into when her father had died, that it would get better.

Meantime…Phinn was just thinking that she might as well get up after all when someone knocked lightly on her door and Ash, bearing a tray, came in.

'Mrs Starkey thought you might like breakfast in bed. I told her I'd bring it up and see how you were.'

'Oh, Ash,' Phinn protested, sitting up and bringing the bed-clothes over her chest. 'Everybody's being so kind.'

'You deserve it,' he replied, and asked, 'Here or on the table?'

'Table,' she answered, thinking, as Ash placed the breakfast tray down on Grandmother Hawkins' table, that she would sit out as soon as he had gone and eat what she could.

'How are you this morning?' Ash asked as he turned back to her.

'Better,' she said.

'Good. I'll leave you to your scrambled egg before it gets cold,' he added, and on impulse bent down and kissed her cheek.

He meant nothing by it other than empathy with the circumstances of her losing her best friend. But the man who had suddenly appeared in the doorway to the side of him did not appear to share the same empathy.

'*Ash!*' he said sharply to his brother.

Phinn looked from one to the other. Never had she known Ty to speak so sharply to him. But, while she was wondering if the two brothers—whom she knew thought the world of each other—were on the point of having a row, Ash did no more than grin at her and say pleasantly, 'Ty,' to his brother.

As Ty stepped into the room, Ash stepped out and closed the door.

'Does Ash usually bring you breakfast in bed?' Ty demanded.

'*Now* what have I done?'

'Apart from showing too much cleavage?' Ty snarled.

Phinn glanced down to where the covers had just a second ago slipped down. Her barely pyjama-top-covered breasts were now on view. 'Had I known I was receiving visitors I'd have worn an overcoat!' she flared, quickly covering herself.

Ty did not care for her sarcasm. That much was plain. 'You're quite obviously feeling better this morning!' he rapped.

Phinn was fed up with him. 'You're never the same two minutes together!' she accused hotly, remembering the way he had tenderly dried her eyes in his study yesterday. 'Is there a purpose to your visit?' she demanded hostilely.

'Not the same as my brother's, clearly!'

'As you once mentioned, Ash has a sensitive side. He brought me breakfast for Mrs Starkey and stayed to ask how I was feeling.'

Ty was unimpressed. 'You just leave him alone!' he ordered.

'Leave him alone?' she echoed.

'I don't want to pick up the pieces when another Hawkins does the dirty on him!'

Phinn stared at Ty in disbelief. Was that what he thought of her? She took a hard pull of breath—that or weep that Ty could say such a thing to her. 'Close the door on your way out!' she ordered imperiously—and, oh, heavens, that was it!

She knew she had angered him when his expression

darkened—and that was before he strode over to the bed. 'I'll go when I'm ready!' he barked, standing threateningly over her.

But in Phinn's view she did not have to sit there and take any more. In a flash she was out of bed and snatching up her robe from the end of it as she went.

'Stay as long as you like!' she snapped. 'I'm off to take a shower.'

Wrong! 'You don't care who you hurt, do you?' Ty snarled, whipping the robe away from her and spinning her round to face him.

Hurt? Him? Hardly likely. He must be referring to Ash. 'You've got a short memory!' she erupted. What had happened to *you're so good with him*?

'Not as short as yours!' Ty grated, and with that he caught a hold of her and pulled her into his arms. 'Less than a week ago you were mine for the taking!' he hurled at her vitriolically. 'Let me remind you!' And, without waiting for permission, he hauled her pyjama-clad body up against him. The next Phinn knew, his mouth was over hers. Not tenderly, not gently, but punishingly, angrily, furiously— and she hated him.

'Let me go!' she hissed, when briefly his mouth left her.

'Like hell,' he scorned, and clamped his lips over hers again. And while holding her in one arm, his other hand pushed the thin straps of her pyjamas vest to one side.

Then his lips were seeking her throat; his hands were in her long flowing hair as he held her still. 'No,' she protested— he took no notice. She pushed at him—that did no good either and in fact only seemed to provoke him further, because his hand left her hair, but only to capture her left breast. 'Don't!' she cried. She ached for his kisses, but not like this.

Ty ignored her 'Don't' but as if enflamed by the feel of her lovely breast in his hold, the next she knew her vest pyjamas top was pulled down about her waist and her pink-tipped breasts were uncovered and Ty was staring at her full creamy breasts as though mesmerised.

He stretched out a hand as though to touch one of those pink peaks and Phinn could not take any more.

'No, Ty,' she cried brokenly. 'Not like this.'

She thought he was going to ignore her, but then it was as though something in her tone had got through to him. Got through to this man who liked to keep his sensitivity well hidden. Because Ty pulled his hand back and stared at her, at the shine of unshed tears in her eyes. And some of his colour seemed to ebb away.

'Oh, God!' was wrenched from him on a strangled kind of sound, and in the next moment he had stepped away from her. A split second later, as if the very hounds of hell were after him, Ty abruptly spun away from her and went striding from the room.

It was the end, and Phinn knew that it was. She had no idea what had driven the civilised man she knew him to be to act in the way he had, and, while she might forgive him, she had an idea—with that agonised *Oh, God!* still ringing in her ears—that it would be a long while before he would be able to forgive himself.

And all, she knew, because of Ash. Ty had been rough on her when he had first known her on account of his protectiveness of Ash. But she had thought Ty had learned that she would never hurt his brother. But, no. Despite what had taken place between her and Ty previously, he had twice witnessed what he had thought to be a tender scene between her and Ash—yesterday, when he had arrived home and had seen Ash with an arm around her, and just now, when he had been passing her open door and had spotted Ash kissing her cheek on an impulse of the moment. As he had said, he feared that another Hawkins would 'do the dirty' on Ash again.

Feeling defeated suddenly, Phinn knew that she was leaving. What was there to stay for? By the look of it, Ty would clap his hands when she went. As he had said himself, when Ash was on form he was good in a crisis. Which meant that since Ash had taken over yesterday, when Ruby had died—tears sprang to her eyes again—Ash was back to his old self and was no longer in need of a companion.

With her appetite gone, Phinn ignored the breakfast tray that Mrs Starkey had so kindly prepared and went and took a shower.

She had almost completed her packing when she heard the sound of a car engine. She went to the window and was in time to see Ty's car being driven out of the gates at the bottom of the drive.

Pain seared her that she would never see Ty again. Not that she had anything that she particularly wanted to say to him, but… Perhaps it was just as well that she left before he got back.

Ten minutes later, acknowledging that she could not take all her luggage with her—not without transport—Phinn remembered how yesterday Ash had offered to drive her anywhere she wanted to go.

Phinn cancelled that thought when she realised that with Ty being so anti he would just love it when he got back to learn that she had made use of Ash to take her and her belongings to Gloucester.

She had no idea how her mother would take her arriving on her doorstep and asking to stay until she had found other accommodation, but, since her mother had stated more than once that she would like her to live with her and Clive, Phinn didn't think she would have any major objection.

Knowing that her mother would most likely cancel her golfing arrangements if she rang her and asked her to come and pick her up, Phinn opted to ring Mickie Yates.

Disappointingly, he was not answering his phone. She

gathered he must be off somewhere on one of his various pursuits. She did think of asking Jimmie Starkey to take her, but that did not seem fair somehow. He was a hard worker, like his wife, and had earned a weekend to himself.

In the end she knew that she would have to try and make it to Gloucester by bus—if buses in Bishops Thornby still ran on a Saturday. Phinn would contact Mickie at some other time to collect the remainder of her belongings for her.

She left the watch Ty had loaned her on her grandmother's table. She gave a shaky sigh as she recalled Ty's kindness in bringing that familiar table up to her room so she should feel more at home. Then, with a last look around her room, she determinedly picked up one suitcase and left her room.

It was with a very heavy heart that she descended the stairs, but she tried to cheer herself up by reminding herself that her stay had only been going to be temporary anyway.

She had just reached the bottom stair, however, and hefted her case down into the hall, when a sound to her left made her jerk her head that way.

Ty! Colour—hot colour—seared her skin. She had thought he had gone out, and that she would never see him again! But her high colour came from remembering that awful scene in her bedroom earlier. 'I thought I saw you driving your car down the drive!' she said witlessly.

He ignored her comment, his eyes glinting when he could not avoid seeing she had luggage. 'Where do you think you're going with that case?' he demanded shortly.

'I'm leaving,' Phinn replied—and waited for his applause.

It did not come. What came was Ty striding forward and hefting her case up and away from her. 'We'll see about that!' he grated, and, leaving her to follow, her suitcase in his grip, he strode from her in the direction of the drawing room.

Phinn hesitated for a second or two, torn between a need to go and—oh—such a hungry yearning need to stay. Her need to stay—if only for a minute or two longer, while Ty presumably sorted her out about something—won.

'As long as you intend to keep your hands to yourself!' she called after him spiritedly, that lippy part of her refusing to die, no matter what.

A moment later she followed. She was unsure what Ty intended to have a go at her about now. All she hoped was that she would be able to get out of there without hitting him again or with her pride intact—preferably both.

CHAPTER NINE

TY HAD not cooled down at all, Phinn observed when she entered the drawing room. Her case was on the floor a yard from him, and he had his back to her, but his expression when he turned to survey her standing there was most definitely hostile.

'You want me to apologise?' he queried, his tone quiet. But hostility was still there lurking, Phinn felt sure.

She shrugged her shoulders. 'Suit yourself,' she replied, and saw that her remark had not sweetened him any.

He walked by her to firmly close the drawing room door, then came back to stand in front of her. And off on some other tack, he demanded, 'Where do you think you're going?'

'Not that it's any business of yours, but—'

'Not my business?' he echoed. 'You waltz in here, disrupt the whole household, and—'

'Now, just a minute!' Love him she might, but she didn't have to take his false accusations. 'For a start, *you* invited me here. Yes, I know I've had an easy ride of it…' Oh, damn. Those tears again, as a fleeting memory of her riding Ruby got to her. She looked down at the carpet while she gathered herself together.

But suddenly Ty had come closer, hostility forgotten. 'Oh, Phinn,' he murmured softly. 'My timing is, as ever, all to pieces where you're concerned. You are grieving for Ruby, and all I'm doing if giving you more grief.'

'Don't be nice to me!' Phinn cried agitatedly. 'When you're wearing your hard-as-blazes hat I can cope, but…'

'But not when I go soft on you?' he queried. 'I shall have to remember that,' he commented—a touch obscurely, Phinn felt, since after today she would not be seeing him again.

'Look, I have to go. I've—er—got a bus to catch.'

'Bus!' He looked scandalised, and let her know how he felt about that in no uncertain tone. 'You can forget that, Phinn Hawkins!' he told her bluntly.

'Ty, please. Look…'

'No, *you* look. I know this isn't the best of times for you. And I know you've had almost a year of one upset after another. And I so admire the way you have battled on. But, at the risk of upsetting you further, I'm afraid I cannot let you leave until we've talked our—problem through. And, whatever happens, you are certainly not going anywhere with that case by bus.'

'I'm—not?' What was there to talk about? Oh, heavens—had he seen her love for him and considered that a 'problem' to be talked through? No way was she talking *that* problem through!

'If you're still set on leaving after—' He broke off, then resumed steadily, 'I'll take you anywhere you want to go. But first come and sit down. I'll get Mrs Starkey to bring us some coffee.'

'I don't want coffee—er—thank you,' Phinn refused primly.

She wasn't sure that she wanted to sit down either. But, taking the chair furthest away from the one she thought he would use, she went and sat. Only to find that Ty, as if wanting to be able to read her expression, had pulled up a chair close by.

'I'm aware I'm in your debt,' she said in a rush. She did not want him reading any unwary, unguarded look in her eyes or face, no matter how fleeting. He was as sharp as a tack was

Ty Allardyce. 'But I intend to get a job. Obviously I'll settle my debt with you as soon as—'

'For God's sake!' Ty burst in. 'Don't you know, after what you did for Ash, that I shall be forever in *your* debt?'

'This is about money. I don't like owing money,' Phinn retaliated, shrugging his comment away. 'Circumstances have caused me to accept you paying the vet…' She bit her lip. Darling Ruby again. 'Look, Ty,' she said abruptly, 'I know that you don't approve of my—er—friendship with Ash. That you fear I might hurt him. But I never would. Trust me, I never would. Apart from Ash not being interested in me in that sort of way—romantically, I mean—I'm not like my cousin…'

'Ash isn't interested in you that way?' Ty immediately took up. And was at his belligerent best, when he barked, 'You could have fooled me!'

'Why? Because you saw him with a sympathetic arm around me yesterday? He's sensitive. You know he is. He guessed I'd got Ruby on my mind this morning—and kissed my cheek in the empathy of the moment.'

'He doesn't normally go around kissing you?'

For heaven's sake! 'He leaves that to you!' Phinn snapped, then realised she did not want to remind him of how he had kissed her before—apart from earlier—and her willingness in that department. 'Look,' she rushed on, starting to feel exasperated, 'I know all this fuss is solely about your protection of Ash, and your fear I'm another avaricious Hawkins ready to hurt him, but I promise you the only way I can hurt him is in the way a sister might unthinkingly hurt her brother.'

Ty's eyebrows shot up. 'You see Ash in a *sisterly* light?' he challenged sceptically, everything about him saying that he did not believe a word of it. And that annoyed her.

'Of course I do! The same way that Ash thinks of me as his honorary sister!'

'He thinks of you as his *sister*?' Ty's disbelief was rife.

'Don't you two ever talk to each other?' Phinn exclaimed.

'Apparently not. Not about our deepest emotions, obviously.'

Phinn guessed it was a 'man thing', because never had she known two brothers so close.

'What makes you so sure that Ash regards you only as a brother would?' Ty challenged.

'Oh, Ty, stop worrying,' Phinn said softly, knowing all Ty's concern was for his brother. 'Ash actually said so one day this week. Besides, Ash has someone new on his mind.'

Ty's head jerked back in surprise. 'You're saying he's interested in somebody else?' he asked, but was soon again looking as though he did not believe it for a moment. 'He didn't so much as glance at Cheryl Wyatt last Saturday, and I invited her especially to…'

'You were matchmaking?' Phinn queried, amazed, her mouth falling open. Ty had invited Cheryl on Ash's account! Phinn's jealousy of the beautiful Cheryl Wyatt eased somewhat. If Ty had invited Cheryl for Ash's benefit, then Ty could not be interested in her for himself. 'Er—wrong stable,' she announced.

'Wrong stable?'

'I don't think I'm breaking any great confidence—Ash has a date with Geraldine Walton tonight.'

It was Ty's turn to be amazed. 'He's…? Geraldine Walton?'

Phinn found she could not hold down a grin. 'So you've no need to worry that I'm going to let Ash down,' she remarked lightly. 'I just don't figure in that way.' Looking at Ty, loving him so much, she truly did not want him worrying any more about his kid brother. 'So you see, Ty, Ash truly sees me as a kind of sister.'

With her glance still on Ty as what she had revealed sank in, Phinn felt that he seemed to visibly relax. As if what she had just said was somehow of the utmost importance. As if a whole load of concern had been lifted from his shoulders. And it was only then that Phinn realised just how tense Ty had been.

Her grin became impish, and she just had to add, 'Sorry, Ty, that sort of makes me your sister too.'

But his reply truly jolted her. Shaking his head, he told her flatly, 'I don't think so. I don't want you for a sister.'

That hurt, but somehow she managed to hide it, and as casually as she could she got to her feet, tears again threatening—but this time tears from the hurt that he had just so carelessly served her. 'Well, that puts me in my place,' she commented offhandedly. And, head up, pride intact, 'Well, if that's it—if that settles your concerns about Ash—I'll be off.'

She did not get very far! To her surprise, she did not even get as far as lifting up her suitcase before Ty was standing in front of her, blocking her way. 'That,' he clipped, 'in no way settles it.'

'It doesn't?'

He moved his head slowly from side to side. 'No, it does not,' he said firmly, to her further surprise. Adding, 'I've a more special place for you than that.'

More special than a sister? Hardly! 'You've heard how good I am in an office? You're offering me a job?'

'There *is* a job for you—if all else fails,' Ty replied.

'What sort of job?' A job where she stood a chance of seeing him again? No, thank you, said her pride. Oh, please, said her heart.

Ty looked at her for long moments, and then stated, 'When Ash goes to Honeysuckle Farm it will be more than a full-time job for him. I shall need an estate manager here.'

'Me?' she exclaimed. But, on thinking about it, 'You won't need anyone full-time,' she denied. 'You're selling Yew Tree Farm, I believe. And while it will take a couple of years for Ash to lick Honeysuckle into shape…' Her voice tailed off, guilt smiting her.

'Honeysuckle will be fine—with your input. Presumably with your local knowledge you know of someone who will show Ash the ropes?'

'Er—I do, actually,' she admitted. 'Old Jack Philips—he's worked on the land all his life. He retired about a year ago, but he's finding retirement irksome. He was saying, that lunchtime Ash and I went to the Cat for a drink, that he's itching to have a few days' work each week.' Ty smiled, and that was so weakening Phinn had to work hard not to wilt. 'But that still doesn't make an estate manager's job here full-time,' she stated firmly. 'Besides, I've no experience of being an estate manager.'

'Sure you have. You take a stroll through the woods and spot exactly which trees need taking out—know which new trees should be planted. You've an in-built sense of country lore. Not to mention you can deal with office work with both hands tied behind your back.'

Phinn had to smile herself. Yes, she could do all of that, and she would love to stay—would love to walk the estate, love to be his estate manager—but there wasn't even a couple of days' work here.

'And don't forget there are a couple of tenanted cottages that would have to be kept up to date—their upkeep and running repairs to be contracted out.'

Phinn shook her head. She didn't want to go, she knew that she didn't, but... 'I have to go,' she said decidedly.

Ty stared at her, not liking what he was hearing. 'It's me, isn't it?' he challenged. But before Phinn could panic too much that he had guessed at her feelings for him, he was going on. 'You've had enough of my grouchy attitude with you on too many occasions?'

'Ty—I...' She was feeling out of her depth suddenly.

'Will you stay if I promise to mend my ways—apologise for every unkind word I ever said? Every—?'

'Oh, Ty,' she cut in. 'You weren't awful all the time!' She laughed lightly, ready to forgive him anything. She guessed that was what love was all about—forgiving hurt, real or imagined. 'Sometimes you have been particularly splendid,' she added, quite without thinking.

'Truly?' he asked, and seemed tense again suddenly. 'I wasn't very pleasant when I kissed you this morning, but—'

'I don't think I want to go there,' Phinn rushed in. 'I—er—was meaning more particularly your thoughtfulness in putting Grandmother Hawkins' table in my room. Getting Mr Timmins in to tune the piano. The—' She broke off. She had been about to say the replacement watch he had bought her—but she did not want to remind him of how her own watch had become waterlogged.

'Do the good times outweigh the bad, Phinn?' he asked.

'Yes, of course they do,' she replied without hesitation. It wasn't his fault that she had fallen in love with him. 'I just don't know what Ruby and I would have done if you hadn't come along and offered us a home.'

'It pales into insignificance when I think of what you did for Ash, and in turn for me.'

'We're going to have to stop this or we'll end up a mutual admiration society,' Phinn said brightly. And then, because she must, 'Thank you, Ty, for letting Ruby end her days in comfort and peace.' So saying, she took a step towards him, stretched up and kissed him.

It was a natural gesture on her part, but when she went to step back again, she discovered that Ty had taken a hold of her hands in his. And, tense still, he asked quietly, 'Am I to take it that you—quite—like me?' looking down into her wide blue eyes.

Phinn immediately looked away. 'You know I like you!' she flared. 'Grief—you think I—' She broke off. 'Time I went!' she said abruptly.

But Ty still had a hold of her hands. 'Not yet,' he countered.

Just that, but there was an assertive kind of firmness in his tone that Phinn found worrying. 'You accused me earlier of not ever talking to my brother. I think, Phinn, that you and I should start talking to each other—openly.'

Phinn was already shaking her head. 'Oh, I don't know about that,' she replied warily.

And Ty smiled a gentle smile, his tension easing as her nervousness increased. 'What are you afraid of?' he asked softly. 'I tell you now, all pretence aside, that while I may have unwittingly hurt you in the past, I will never knowingly hurt you again.' Her throat went dry. She tried to swallow. 'Come and sit down with me,' he went on. She shook her head, but found that Ty was leading her over to a sofa anyway. She still hadn't found her voice when, seated beside her, Ty turned to her and stated, 'Given that I was such a brute to you when we first met, you have a very forgiving nature, Phinn.'

'Brute doesn't cover it!' She was glad her vocal cords were working—thanks largely to Ty going off the subject of her liking him.

'I agree,' he conceded, his grey eyes steady on hers. 'To recap, and in my defence, Ash was doing so well here on his own, and I was going through a busy time in London. The obvious thing to do was to leave matters down here with him. The alterations were going well, with no need for me to try and find time to pay a visit, but when I did find time to come home I was shocked to my core by Ash's appearance—at how ill he looked.'

'You must have been. I was myself,' Phinn volunteered. 'He told you about Leanne?'

'I got most of it from Mrs Starkey. I supposed I grilled her pretty thoroughly. When she'd told me all that she could, I was in no mood to be pleasant to any member of the Hawkins family.'

'You ordered me off your land.'

'And to my dying day I shall ever be grateful that you ignored me bossing you about and came back again.'

Phinn had an almost overwhelming urge to kiss him again, but reckoned that she had done enough of that already. And in any case, he already knew that she liked him without her giving this clever man more to work on.

'I think you first started to get to me that day by the pool,' he went on when she said nothing. 'I could see you were upset about something, for all it didn't stop you being lippy, but I had no idea then that you were in shock.'

'I—er—started to get to you? You—er—started to like me, you mean?'

Ty stilled. 'It matters to you that I like you?' he enquired quietly.

She shrugged. She was getting good at it. 'Everybody likes to be liked,' she answered—and thankfully he let it go.

'It was more a personal thing for me,' Ty said carefully.

'Oh,' she murmured. Oh—heavens!

'And the more I got to know you, the more I got to like you,' Ty went on.

Her throat went dry again. 'Oh—really?' she managed, but her voice was quite croaky and unlike her own. She coughed to clear it, and was able to offer an offhand kind of, 'That's good.'

'Not from where I was seeing it,' Ty answered. She refused to say *oh* again. 'From where I was seeing it,' he continued, unprompted, 'that's when the trouble began.'

'Trouble?'

'Trouble.' He nodded. 'There was I, getting to like you more and more each time I saw you. And there were you, my dear Phinn, excelling in the job I hired you to do. Ash was coming on in leaps and bounds. So much so that you, as his companion, were doing things with him that I—I found I wanted to do with you.'

Phinn blinked. Open-mouthed, she stared. 'Really?' she gasped.

'Believe it,' Ty replied. 'I found I was coming back here every chance I could.'

'Because of Ash, of course.'

Ty smiled. 'Of course,' he answered. 'So, if it's all about Ash, why do I want you to take me fishing too—to teach me to tie a fly—to take me with you sketching? And why, heaven knows why, do I feel so cranky when Ash tells me that you think he's gorgeous?'

Phinn could only stare at Ty in amazement. 'You wanted me to think—you—were gorgeous too?' She didn't believe it.

'I think I'd have settled for kind, or nice—or even for half of the smiles you sent my brother's way.'

Phinn stared at him, feeling somewhat numbed. Her brain seemed to have seized up anyway. 'You—were...?' The words would not come. She dared not say it—and make a fool of herself.

'Jealous,' Ty supplied. 'The word you're looking for is jealous.'

'No!' she denied faintly, not believing it.

'Yes,' Ty contradicted.

'I—er—expect that—um—happens with brothers. A sort of brotherly—er—thing,' Phinn said faintly, not having the first clue about it, but still not believing that Ty meant what it sounded as if he meant.

'I don't know about that. I've never been jealous of Ash before. In fact, I grew up with it being second nature for me to look out for him, to protect him if need be.' Ty took a long-drawn breath then, but continued firmly. 'Which is why it threw me when I realised my rush to get home as soon as I could was not so much to check on how he was doing, but more because I wanted to see you.'

Phinn's eyes widened, and her throat went dry again. 'No,' she murmured.

'True,' Ty replied. 'You always seemed to be having fun

with Ash. I wanted to stay home and have fun with you too.' And, while Phinn stared at him stunned, 'Work was losing its appeal,' he confessed.

She found that staggering! She had formed an impression that Ty lived, slept and dreamed work. 'You...' she managed faintly.

'I,' he replied, 'knew I was in trouble.'

'Trouble?' she echoed witlessly.

And Ty smiled a gentle bone-melting smile for her as he explained, 'At the start I wanted you here in my home for Ash. But the more I had to do with you, and the more I knew of you, the more—dear Phinn—I wanted you in my home not for Ash, but for me.'

She swallowed, her insides a total disaster. 'Oh,' she said huskily.

'And it was *oh*,' Ty said gently. 'Because of how Ash was, he had to be my first concern. He liked you, the two of you got on well—which was fine. What was not fine was that the two of you should start to care for each other. That,' he said, 'was not what I wanted.'

'You were protecting Ash when you were anti me?'

Ty looked at her steadily. 'Where you were concerned, Phinn, I was losing it.' And, as she stared at him, 'I was as jealous as hell where you two were concerned,' he owned. 'Logic fast disappearing.'

'Logic?' She suddenly seemed incapable of stringing two words together.

'Logic,' he agreed, explaining, 'I knew, logically, that there was absolutely no sense at all in my not returning to London on a Sunday evening—but there was no space in my head for logic when it came to my persistent need to want to be where you were.'

'Oh, Ty!' Phinn murmured. He had delayed his departure because of her! She found that staggering, and had to make one gigantic effort to get herself together—she owned she was in pieces. 'Look, I—um—know you're a bit averse to me leaving, but you don't have to—'

'Haven't you been listening to a word I've been saying?' Ty cut in sharply. 'No, I don't want you to leave. But that's only a part of it. You're in my head, in my—'

'No!' she denied—but that was when her memory awoke and gave her one mighty sharp poke. 'If you're going on to—' She broke off, running out of steam before she began. But, gaining her second wind, she snatched her hands out of his grasp, the better to be able to tell him, 'You had your chance with me once, Tyrell Allardyce. If you think you can sweet-talk me—only to reject me again—you've got another—'

'Reject you?' Ty cut in, staring at her, thunderstruck. 'When did I ever reject you?'

'You've got a short memory!' She had an idea she had gone a bit pink, but had to have her say. 'Less than a week ago, up in your bedroom, I wasn't sophisticated enough for you. You—'

'For God's sake.' Ty chopped her off. 'I was off my head with desire for you!'

Her colour was definitely pink—high pink—and she began to wish she had not brought the subject up.

'Oh, Phinn, you idiot. Not sophisticated enough? Don't you know I treasure your innocence?' She shook her head, but Ty caught a hold of her hands and hung on to them when she struggled. 'Listen to me,' he urged. 'That night—last Sunday night,' he inserted, to show he had not forgotten a thing, 'I was already in a situation where I was more feeling than thinking. And then you go and throw a bombshell at me, and I've moved on to a totally new situation. I needed to be able to think clearly—but, dammit, I couldn't.'

'Hmph!' she scorned. 'What was there to think about?'

'Oh, Phinn—you, my love.' Her spine was in meltdown again. 'If you'll forgive me, we were both highly emotionally charged. I needed a few moments of space to think what was best *for you*.'

'For me?'

'Sweet Phinn,' Ty said gently, 'I knew I had to be away by four in the morning. Was unsure of exactly when I'd be back. I needed to be able to think, to judge—was it too soon to tell you how much you mean to me? How would you react if I did? I didn't seem to know very much any more. What I did know was that I wanted what was best for you. But did I have enough time to hold you in my arms and make you understand how very special you are to me? Fear gripped me—would I scare you away if I tried?'

'Special?' Phinn whispered, her throat choked. She gave a dry cough. 'Special?'

'Very special,' Ty answered. 'You were at your most vulnerable—I didn't want to go leaving you with any doubts. But before I have the chance to think it through, you and your massive pride are up in arms, and you're more or less telling me to forget it—and thereby solving my quandary for me.'

Phinn's head was in a whirl. 'Er—as you mentioned—we—er—should—perhaps—have talked a little more openly.' And, getting herself more together, 'Though since you went away there hasn't been any chance to…'

'I wanted to phone you. On Monday. On Tuesday. Countless times I had the phone in my hand—' He broke off to ask sharply, 'Has Will Wyatt been in touch?' And, when she was not quick enough to answer, 'I'll take that as a yes. He's been angling for an invite here all week. But…' Suddenly Ty halted. Abruptly—as if he had just reached the end of his rope. 'I'm done with talking,' he said impatiently. And then, taking what seemed to her to be a steadying breath, he said, 'Just tell me straight—if I promise not to roll in the aisle laughing, will you stand up with me in church and say "I, Delphinnium Hawkins, take you, Tyrell Allardyce"?'

On the instant, searing hot colour rushed to her face. She could not think, could not breathe. Though as Phinn recalled how Ty had said he did not want her for a sister, that he had a more special place for her than that, so her brain started to stir. He wanted her—not as a sister, but as his wife! Feeling stunned, for countless seconds Phinn could only stare at him. She had never for a moment dreamt that that special place was this! And, feeling winded, she was not even sure that she could credit having heard what she thought she had just heard.

Had Ty, in effect, just asked her to marry him? She felt trembly all over, but with her heart beating wildly she could not just leave it there. Staring wide-eyed at Ty, she saw he looked tense again—seemed to be waiting. He had asked a question and was waiting, tensely, for her reply!

Phinn took a deep breath. 'What...?' she began. But her voice let her down. She swallowed, and found her voice again. 'What sort of pr-proposal is that to make to a girl?' she asked with what breath she could find—and waited for him to roar with laughter because she had totally misunderstood.

But no! Looking at him—and her eyes were fixed solely on his face—she saw that he was looking nowhere but at her either. She saw him take another steadying breath, and came as near to fainting as she had ever done in her life when, after a moment of searching her face, Ty solemnly answered, 'Hopefully, should I be able to clear away my fears over you and Ash, the proposal I wanted to make—the one I rehearsed in ten different ways, but feared that you might laugh at— goes...' He paused to take a deep pull of breath. 'Goes: Phinn Hawkins, I love you so very much that I cannot bear to be away from you. I...'

'You—love—me?' Phinn whispered.

'I love you so very much, my darling Phinn,' Ty confirmed. 'Love you so that you are in my head night and day. You fill my dreams. Everywhere I go, you go too. You are there in every-thing I do—and it is my most earnest wish that you marry me.'

Ooh! The breath seemed to leave her body on a sigh. Numbly, she stared at him. He loved her! Ty—the man she loved—loved her. She stared at him, her breath taken.

'Well?' he asked when she said nothing, his hands gripping hers tightly. 'Have you no answer for me?'

Oh, Ty. Didn't he know? She tried to speak, but no sound came. She tried again, and this time managed to answer, 'I'm—not laughing.'

Her words were faint, but Ty heard them. 'That gives me hope,' he said.

'You *are* serious?' She started to have doubts.

'Loving you is not something I would joke about.'

'I'm sorry,' she apologised, her voice gaining strength. 'Your—er—what you've just said is such a surprise.'

'Is it?' Ty seemed surprised himself that she had not seen how things were with him. But his patience was getting away from him; tension and strain were showing in his face. 'Please, Phinn, give me an answer,' he urged.

She smiled at him, her answer there in her all-giving tender smile as she replied, 'If you don't mind if I whisper the "Delphinnium" bit in church, there is nothing I would like better than to take you, Tyrell Allardyce.'

Ty did not wait to hear any more. Joyously he gathered her into his arms and tenderly kissed her. 'I didn't make a mistake. That *was* a yes I heard?' he pulled back to ask—and Phinn realised that Ty, like her, could hardly believe his hearing.

'Oh, yes,' she replied softly.

'You love me?'

'I was afraid you would guess.'

'Say it?' he encouraged, with love for her in his eyes.

'Oh, Ty, I love you so,' she whispered.

'Darling Phinn,' he breathed, and, drawing her closer, he

kissed her lingeringly. For a short while he seemed content to just hold her like that, close up to his heart. Then, 'How long have you known that you didn't just hate me, as I deserve?'

'You're fishing,' she accused.

'Why not?' He grinned. 'I've been a soul in torment.'

'About me?' she asked, her eyes widening.

'Who else? I asked you to stay here partly because there was nothing I would not do for the woman who saved my brother's life, and partly out of concern that Ash would brood on his unhappiness if I left him here on his own. Only to soon find that, when I should be rejoicing because Ash is staring to pull out of it, I'm a bit put out at the closeness the two of you seem to be sharing. I denied, of course, that I was in any way jealous.'

'Oh, heavens!' Phinn gasped.

'You noticed I was out of sorts?' Ty asked, kissing her because he had to.

Phinn sighed lovingly. 'I thought you were anti because you'd seen how well Ash and I were getting on and were afraid that another Hawkins was getting to him.'

'It wasn't so much you getting to him that was concerning me, but that he might be getting to you.'

'You *were* jealous!' she exclaimed.

'I acknowledged that on the day I found you in the music room. I held you in my arms—and wanted to hold you again.'

'You did hold me again. That same night—in the stable,' Phinn recalled.

'I was ready to grab at the smallest excuse,' Ty replied.

Phinn smiled at him. 'That was the night I realised that I was in love with you,' she confessed.

'Then?' Ty exclaimed.

'I tried to hide it.'

'You succeeded. Although…'

'Although?' Phinn queried, when it seemed as though Ty would leave it there.

'Last Sunday—in my bedroom—when you were so unbe-lievably giving to me…well, it gave me hope. All this week I've been tormented by visions of you, wanting to phone, afraid to phone. Had I read too much into your unawakened but eager response to me? Was it just some sort of awakening chemistry on your part? Or dared I hope—did you care for me?'

'What did you decide?'

Ty smiled. 'That was the problem. I couldn't decide—and it was driving me mad. I decided to get back home as fast as I could, the sooner to find out.' He gently stroked the side of her face. 'It was inappropriate for me to say anything yester-day, when you were in such distress over Ruby.'

'I'm sorry I hit you.'

Ty kissed her. 'Given that you pack a powerful punch, I thoroughly deserved it. I was as immediately appalled by what I had said as you were,' he revealed. 'I knew I had to leave matters until the morning—this morning—when I would try to gauge how things were and then, if the signs were good, put myself out of my misery by telling you how things were with me, hoping against hope that there was a chance for me with you.'

'It all went sort of wrong,' Phinn put in.

'You can say that again. I wanted to come to your room last night—and again this morning—to check how you were. I wanted to hold and comfort you. But, knowing how you in your scanty pyjamas can trigger off physical urges in me, I was unsure. Having managed to stay away, I was a little short of incensed when I saw your bedroom door was open, and as I look in as I'm passing, there's my brother, kissing you.'

'He was just being his lovely self.'

'I know, and I'm ashamed,' Ty confessed. 'Ashamed that I was for an instant jealous of him. And oh, so heartily ashamed of my behaviour with you afterwards.' Phinn leaned forward and tenderly kissed him. 'Forgive me?' he asked.

'Of course,' she replied, smiling, loving him, her heart full to overflowing.

'Ash knew in your room this morning that I was jealous—the wretch,' Ty said good-humouredly. 'I can see that now. Now that I know his interests lie in other directions, I can forgive him that he went off whistling, not a care in the world—leaving me stewing when I sent him off to Yew Tree Farm with some paperwork.'

'He took your car.'

'He can be very aggravating when the mood's on him,' Ty complained indulgently, his love for his brother obvious. And Phinn knew that Ty was heartily glad to have his brother back to his old self, no matter how occasionally aggravating he might be. 'So—having got Ash out of the way, having got the house to myself—I'm left waiting for you to come down, knowing that I want to marry you, if you'll have me, but still with concerns about how Ash feels about you and how you feel about Ash.'

'And I came down with my case packed.'

'I wasn't having that,' Ty answered, smiling. 'Whatever the consequences. I knew my timing was off, knew you were upset, but I had no more time to wait. I've loved you too long, darling Phinn, to be able to let you walk out of my door.'

'Oh, Ty,' she sighed, and loved and kissed him. She pulled back to ask softly, 'When did you know?'

'That I loved you?' He looked at her lovingly. 'I suppose you could say that the writing was on the wall when I ignored the social events I normally enjoy in London the sooner to get back here.'

'For Ash?' she inserted.

'Of course for Ash.' Ty grinned. 'Then, as Ash began to surface from his feelings of desolation and I saw that a bond was growing between you and him, I found myself thinking that if Ash was ready to join the dating circuit again, I'd find him somebody to date. I realised then that I had begun to think of you as *my* Phinn, and that in fact I was actually in love with you.'

Her heart was so full, Phinn just beamed a smile at him. 'Oh,' she sighed. And was kissed. And kissed in return. 'You—um—mentioned inviting Cheryl Wyatt...?'

'Much good did it do me!'

'It didn't do me much good either,' Phinn owned. And, when Ty looked a touch puzzled, 'Being jealous is not your sole prerogative,' she confessed.

'Honestly?'

'No need to look so delighted.'

'I'm ashamed,' he lied with a grin. 'Anyhow, that backfired on me, didn't it? There am I, hoping Ash might show an interest in Cheryl, not knowing that he was keen to date Geraldine Walton...'

'I almost mentioned how well Ash had been getting on with Geraldine that night I asked you if it was all right if I took a part-time job—only the moment passed.'

'I wish you *had* mentioned it,' Ty commented feelingly, and Phinn, realising that he must have known some mighty anguish over her and his brother, wished now that she had told him too, and Ty went on, 'Anyway, with Ash so much brighter than he had been, I invited the Wyatts—only to find it's not Ash I've paired up, and if I'm not careful my friend Will will be marching off with you.' Ty broke off, and then, taking her face in his hands, 'Oh, sweet love, have you any idea what I feel for you?' There was such a wealth of love for her in his tone that Phinn felt too choked to be able to speak. 'While you charmed everyone at dinner last Saturday, I looked at you, could not seem to take my eyes off you, and I have never felt so mesmerised.'

'I had to keep looking at you too,' Phinn confessed huskily.

They kissed and held each other. And then Ty was saying, 'So why do I find you entertaining Will Wyatt in Ruby's stable? You don't mind talking about Ruby?'

Phinn shook her head. 'I don't want her forgotten. She's been a part of me for so long.' Swallowing down an emotional moment, she said, 'Will Wyatt was outside smoking a cigar when I nipped out.'

'Cursed swine,' Ty said cheerfully. 'He stuck to you like glue as much as he could—Saturday *and* Sunday.'

Phinn laughed. 'I—er—take it you didn't give in to him angling for an invitation to Broadlands again?'

'Too true,' Ty answered ruefully. And, after a moment, 'Though I shall be delighted to invite him to our wedding.' Her breath caught, and Ty's expression changed to one of concern. 'You *are* going to marry me?' he asked urgently.

'Oh, Ty…' As if there was any doubt. 'I'd love to marry you.'

He breathed a heartfelt sigh. 'Good,' he said, but added, 'And soon?'

'Um…' was as far as she got before they both saw his car sail past the window.

'Right,' Ty commented decisively. 'First we'll tell that brother of mine that I'd like him to be my best man.' He looked at her to see if she had any objection—she beamed her approval. Ash was her brother too—that would be cemented on her marriage to Ty. 'Then we'll drive to Gloucester to see your mother.'

'We're going to see my mother?'

Ty nodded. 'My PA got married last year. Her wedding, with her mother's help, was eighteen months in the planning. I'm afraid, darling Phinn, I can't wait that long to make you Delphinnium Allardyce. We'll go and see your mother and hope to get her approval for a wedding before this month is out.'

'Ty!' Phinn exclaimed, her heart racing. Ty wanted them to be married in less than three weeks' time! Oh—oh, how very, beautifully wonderful!

'You're not objecting? You don't mind?' he pressed swiftly.

Phinn shook her head. 'Not a bit,' she answered dreamily.

'Good, my lovely darling,' Ty breathed. 'Ash may not need you any longer, but I cannot live without you.'

And with that he drew her closer to him and kissed her.

He was still holding her close when the door opened and Ash stood there. He at once saw them—Phinn in his brother's arms, Ty with a look of supreme happiness about him—and a grin suddenly split Ash's face from ear to ear.

'What's this?' he asked, grinning still.

'Come in.' Ty grinned back. 'Come in and say hello to your soon-to-be sister—by marriage.'

REQUEST YOUR FREE BOOKS!
2 FREE NOVELS PLUS 2
FREE GIFTS!

HARLEQUIN® Romance®

From the Heart, For the Heart

YES! Please send me 2 FREE Harlequin® Romance novels and my 2 FREE gifts (gifts are worth about $10). After receiving them, if I don't wish to receive any more books, I can return the shipping statement marked "cancel". If I don't cancel, I will receive 6 brand-new novels every month and be billed just $3.84 per book in the U.S. or $4.24 per book in Canada. That's a savings of 15% off the cover price! It's quite a bargain! Shipping and handling is just 50¢ per book in the U.S. and 75¢ per book in Canada.* I understand that accepting the 2 free books and gifts places me under no obligation to buy anything. I can always return a shipment and cancel at any time. Even if I never buy another book, the two free books and gifts are mine to keep forever.

116 HDN E4GY 316 HDN E4HC

Name	(PLEASE PRINT)	
Address		Apt. #
City	State/Prov.	Zip/Postal Code

Signature (if under 18, a parent or guardian must sign)

Mail to the **Harlequin Reader Service:**
IN U.S.A.: P.O. Box 1867, Buffalo, NY 14240-1867
IN CANADA: P.O. Box 609, Fort Erie, Ontario L2A 5X3

Not valid for current subscribers to Harlequin Romance books.

**Are you a subscriber to Harlequin Romance books
and want to receive the larger-print edition?
Call 1-800-873-8635 today!**

* Terms and prices subject to change without notice. Prices do not include applicable taxes. Sales tax applicable in N.Y. Canadian residents will be charged applicable provincial taxes and GST. Offer not valid in Quebec. This offer is limited to one order per household. All orders subject to approval. Credit or debit balances in a customer's account(s) may be offset by any other outstanding balance owed by or to the customer. Please allow 4 to 6 weeks for delivery. Offer available while quantities last.

Your Privacy: Harlequin Books is committed to protecting your privacy. Our Privacy Policy is available online at www.eHarlequin.com or upon request from the Reader Service. From time to time we make our lists of customers available to reputable third parties who may have a product or service of interest to you. If you would prefer we not share your name and address, please check here. ☐

Help us get it right—We strive for accurate, respectful and relevant communications. To clarify or modify your communication preferences, visit us at www.ReaderService.com/consumerschoice.

HRIO